P9-DCO-157

Can changing your **name**
change your **destiny**?

Now it is the morning of David Bruce Schumacher's sixteenth birthday—and in a sudden, unusual spurt of boldness he has finally made up his mind to just go ahead and *do* it. Although he hasn't discussed it with anyone, he has been thinking about this thing for a long time, toying with the idea but never seriously—never really believing he would actually follow through. Because it's crazy—if not altogether crazy, at least slightly crazy. Yes, it is definitely slightly crazy, and that is partly what makes it so appealing: On this very day, David Bruce Schumacher decides he will officially change his name. . . .

other books by norma howe

IN WITH THE OUT CROWD

GOD, THE UNIVERSE, AND HOT FUDGE SUNDAES

The adventures of Blue Avenger

norma howe

Harper
tempest

An Imprint of HarperCollins*Publishers*

Grateful acknowledgment is made for permission to reprint the following:
"An appointment in Samarra" is from *Sheepey*, by W. Somerset Maugham.
Copyright © 1933 by W. Somerset Maugham.
Used by permission of Doubleday, a division of Random House, Inc.

The Adventures of Blue Avenger

Copyright © 1999 by Norma Howe
All rights reserved. No part of this book may be used or reproduced in any manner
whatsoever without written permission except in the case of brief quotations
embodied in critical articles and reviews. Printed in the United States of America.
For information address HarperCollins Children's Books, a division of HarperCollins
Publishers, 1350 Avenue of the Americas, New York, NY 10019.
Published in Canada by Fitzhenry & Whiteside Ltd.
Reprinted by arrangement with Henry Holt and Company Inc.

Library of Congress Cataloging-in-Publication Data
Howe, Norma.
   The adventures of Blue Avenger : a novel / Norma Howe.
      p.   cm.
   Summary: On his sixteenth birthday, still trying to cope with the unexpected death
of his father, David Schumacher decides—or does he—to change his name to Blue
Avenger, hoping to find a way to make a difference in his Oakland neighborhood and
in the world.
   ISBN 0-06-447225-6 (pbk.)
   [1. Free will and determinism—Fiction.   2. Conduct of life—Fiction.
3. Heroes—Fiction.]   I. Title.
PZ7.H8376 Ad   2000   99-57779
[Fic]—dc21

❖

First Harper Tempest edition, 2000

Friends, Relations, Buckaroos:
Your name here?
This book's for youse.

```
N P S E I L U J C C
E A E C N D I R L H
S U M A J Y A Z P R
S L A R A M A M U I
A A J L U C K W R S
L P T O M L P I E S
L A T S E A A E H U
E T E A T R L N E R
B R R O S A O N A E
A K E E P N M A R G
T C V I B N A E T N
E A E A B O B J S I
D J O N A D R O I G
```

author's note

If it weren't for a chance encounter in the Nevada desert several years ago between the author and a personage who can be referred to only as "Randall the Third," this book could not have been written in its present form. Caught in a compromising situation not far from the infamous Area 51, Randall the Third ("Don't call me Randy!") agreed to disclose some of the information gleaned by members of his so-called clan through the utilization of their highly secret futuristic technology. Predicting the future and rediscovering minutiae from the past with uncanny accuracy seemed to be routine stuff for this tightly knit fifty-seven-member organization. In addition, the author was allowed limited access to the results of their meticulously conducted studies and surveys concerning every subject imaginable. Randall the Third stressed the fact that his unnamed group was not connected with any Earth-based government in any way. His emphasis was on the term *Earth based*. Despite repeated attempts to reconnect with Randall, the author has never seen or heard from him again.

one

Scientists say that in human males, a single seminal emission contains something in the neighborhood of 300 million spermatozoa. Given the task of counting 300 million spermatozoa and counting nonstop at the rate of one sperm cell per second, it would take a bleary-eyed tabulator exactly nine years, 185 days, five hours, and twenty minutes to complete the job. Sperm cells are very tiny, of course—so tiny, in fact, that with a small eyedropper and lots of patience, 2,500 of them could be placed on the dot of this *i*.

(The above quotation is from a new high school biology textbook called *B Is for Biology*. However, this book will not be approved by the state curriculum committee when it meets next year because the majority of members will say that its "tone is too breezy.")

So, how many spermatozoa belonging to Police Officer Walter J. Schumacher took off lickety-split toward the waiting egg of Sally Schumacher on a mild April evening sixteen years and nine months ago? Well, even though no one counted, the actual figure was 319,730,929, which was a few million above average—but Officer Walter Schumacher was healthy and in the prime of life. The lucky spermatozoon that did the trick was number 14,889,004, which was truly miraculous, since the resulting baby turned out to be David Bruce Schumacher, destined to be the unlikely hero of San Pablo High. Amazing as it sounds, no other spermatozoon could have accomplished that feat.

When David was six years old, a similar event occurred, in its own way just as miraculous. This time the resulting baby was his brother, Josh—pesky, sometimes funny, always exasperating—a perfect fit in the "little brother" mold.

And then, seven years after Josh was born, on yet another April evening, Officer Walter J. Schumacher became a tragic statistic—the 1,673rd person in the state of California to die in an automobile accident since the start of the year. Who was to blame? What was the cause? Could it have been a double-dip rocky road ice-cream cone and a tiny brown spider? Well, yes—partly. Along with the billions and billions of other events that led up to the accident, the ice-cream cone and the spider could in all fairness be singled out for blame. For if only Officer Schumacher had not stopped to buy the ice-cream cone on his way home from the police station that evening, the crash would never have happened; or if only the spider had not decided at the precise moment he did to take a hike across the windshield of the other car involved in the accident, momentarily distracting the driver, again, the crash would never have happened. But then, if Officer Schumacher had not spotted the empty parking place right smack in front of the Baskin-Robbins, he would never have stopped. So what about the woman who had vacated the parking space forty-six seconds before Officer Schumacher came along? Was she partly to blame? Why hadn't she taken the time to try on just one more dress at the Bon Marché? And consider the driver of the other car—if only he would have sprayed his garage for spiders as his wife had asked him instead of spending all Saturday afternoon watching the game—ah, yes. If only, if only—but into each life some rain must fall, and no one knows when his own private storm will break. But, some would say, two unanswered questions remain: If things are not counted, can they still be numbered? And do spiders really *decide* to take hikes, or do they just start walking without knowing what in the *#%! they're doing?

Now it is the morning of David Bruce Schumacher's sixteenth birthday—and in a sudden, unusual spurt of boldness he has finally made up his mind to just go ahead and *do* it. Although he hasn't discussed it with anyone, he has been thinking about this thing for a long time, toying with the idea but never seriously—never really believing he would actually follow through. Because it's crazy—if not altogether crazy, at least slightly crazy. Yes, it is definitely slightly crazy, and that is partly what makes it so appealing: On this very day, David Bruce Schumacher decides, he will officially change his name to The Blue Avenger.

The Blue Avenger is a name (or sobriquet, as some might say) he had dreamt up three years before for a cartoon character he had begun to draw in his loneliness and misery after the ice-cream cone and spider mysteriously joined forces to end his father's life. David had wandered out to the garage to look for something— something of his father's, he didn't know quite what— and there he discovered his dad's blue fishing vest stuffed behind a cardboard box containing motor oil, old rags, and a bottle of Windex. David brought the vest into his room and shut the door. His mother was still at work and Josh was at a friend's, so he was all alone in the house. He held his father's vest up by the shoulders and looked at it for several minutes before slipping his arms through the holes and zipping it up. It was a perfect fit. He closed his eyes and suddenly felt almost whole again. Then he sat down at his desk and started to draw.

David wasn't sure how or why he chose the name The Blue Avenger for his cartoon hero back then, except that he had always loved the word *blue*, and the color of the vest most certainly played a part. As for Avenger, well, it had such a nice daredevil sound to it—completely different from the placid and studious *David*. Soon he was spending hours alone in his room, sketching in his amateurish way the imaginary exploits of what turned out to be his own alter ego, filling his private notebooks with multipaneled strips he called "The Adventures of The Blue Avenger." For his stunning and eye-popping feats, The Blue Avenger always wore a blue fishing vest and a blue terry cloth towel secured on his head with a piece of rope in the style of an Arab kaffiyeh (although at the time, David didn't know the proper name for that particular headdress, having just seen and admired it greatly in a movie video his mother rented called *Lawrence of Arabia*).

His very first four-panel strip dealt with the problem of death. He drew The Blue Avenger cornering Death Incarnate, a menacing figure in a black cape with huge, clawlike tentacles. In the last panel, The Blue Avenger has fearlessly ripped off Death's black cape, revealing underneath a sniveling little coward begging for mercy in his filthy underwear.

The problem of the proliferation of injury and death by handguns had become almost an obsession with David after his father had come *that close* to being killed by a handgun the year before his tragic auto accident. So it's not surprising that one of David's favorite themes was The Blue Avenger's ongoing battle for the total elimination of handguns in America. But somehow the bad guys were forever coming up with nasty schemes to foil all of The Blue Avenger's valiant attempts to alleviate this serious problem.

Since Officer Walter Schumacher was a righteous and morally conservative man, he had made a point of explaining to his sons his own feelings regarding the use of swearwords and vulgar language. Profane and obscene language, Officer Schumacher said, demonstrated nothing more nor less than extremely bad manners on the part of the user—like changing a baby's smelly messy diaper at the dinner table, for instance, or picking your nose and then depositing the disgusting yellow globules of snot on your plate for all to see.

As his father intended, those vivid images stayed with David, and, being a decent kid at heart, he consciously chose the more refined road, deciding not to curse or use foul words himself—which immediately made him stand out like a sore thumb among his peers. And when strong or indelicate language was called for by certain unsavory characters in his comic strip, he would imitate the comic books he found in his grandmother's basement and substitute asterisks, pound signs, percent signs, and exclamation points in place of the actual words, which tended to give his cartoons a kind of quaint, old-fashioned, and endearing quality.

And yet another unanswered question remains: Did David in fact consciously *choose* the more refined road of language, or—because of every past experience of his life, the particular set of genes with which he was born, the exact chemical makeup of his brain at the time of this "decision," and various other reasons—was it the only road he was *able* to take?

David was still lying in bed and had not yet opened his eyes at the time that his monumental name-changing brainstorm occurred, which was exactly four minutes and thirty-five seconds before the beep-beep-beep of his digital alarm, set for his usual weekday wake-up hour of 7 A.M. on the dot.

The fact that he was awake but *had not yet opened his eyes* held a curious fascination for David, since he had been aware of an interesting phenomenon since he was quite young: Namely, when he awoke naturally—without the aid of an alarm or other outside disturbance—his eyes remained *closed* until he consciously opened them;

however, on those occasions when he was aroused by an auditory or physical assault upon his body (like his little brother, for instance, shouting or throwing small objects at him), his eyes invariably shot open the way a child's doll is designed to do when it is suddenly raised to an upright position. (Given the choice, he would prefer to wake with his eyes still closed, since it was much more pleasant and conducive to thought.) Nevertheless, the fact that he was even aware of such a thing was only one more of the many idiosyncrasies that tended to set David apart from the other guys in his class. Another was the fact that he had read and understood eighty-seven books from his father's bookshelf in the three years since his death, starting with Daniel Defoe's *Robinson Crusoe*—his father's own early adolescent favorite—and including such varied works as Mark Twain's *Letters from the Earth* and a modern fiction masterpiece by Nicholson Baker titled *The Mezzanine*. At first, David had just picked the books that looked the most interesting, but lately he had begun to finish the task he had given himself in a systematic way, taking the books as they came (from the top shelf down, and left to right). The next book in line was Lewis Thomas's *The Lives of a Cell*; then came

Appointment in Samarra, by John O'Hara; and a thick, dog-eared travel book called *A Complete Travel Guide to Rome*, on page twenty-three of which there appears a photograph of the statue of Giordano Bruno, which stands in the center of a Roman square called the Campo dei Fiori, and the following description:

> In the center of the *Campo dei Fiori* (meaning "field of flowers") there stands a haunting, brooding statue of Giordano Bruno, a sixteenth-century philosopher and heretic, who was burned at the stake on this very spot by the Inquisition on 17 February 1600 because he refused to recant his belief that the sun is the center of our planetary system and that the universe is infinite. Credited with inspiring the European liberal movements of the nineteenth century, particularly the Italian movement for national political unity, Bruno is also regarded by many as a martyr for the cause of intellectual freedom.

When he finishes reading about Rome, David will have only twenty-seven more books to go. After reading the books his father had read, David hopes to have a better understanding of him and of his philosophy of life. Officer Schumacher had no sympathy whatsoever for the criminal elements of society with whom he came in daily contact, and he often repeated to David his view that "human beings are wholly responsible for their own actions, no ifs, ands, or buts!" David, however, was not convinced that this was the case, and that was his dilemma.

Some of David's best thoughts have come to him during those early morning moments upon first awakening. On some mornings he would plan out entire episodes for The Blue Avenger, but lately he realized he hadn't been thinking as much about his comic strip character as in former days. For the past several weeks his early morning thoughts had usually been centered around the new girl at school, Omaha Nebraska Brown, and the wonderfully complex and subtle differences between love and lust.

But this morning, after the breath-quickening flush of excitement caused by the name-changing decision had subsided, he knew he wouldn't have time to do justice to Omaha. So instead he pondered briefly on The

Question—that same haunting, persistent, obsessive, and recurrent question that had plagued him for years: Does free will truly exist? Do we actually have *choices* in this life (as his father so firmly believed) or are our every thought and action the necessary result of the physical laws of the universe, *independent* of our will?

There has to be a way to figure this out, David thought. What about my eyes? They're still closed. So, am I going to open them exactly when *I* choose to, or are they going to open according to some predetermined plan over which I have no control? How can I test that? There must be a way!

David thought and thought. Well, okay, he decided finally. Here's what I'll do. I'll count to five, and then I'll open my eyes. I'm completely in control here. I'm the captain of my own destiny, and after the count of five, I *shall* open my eyes. He swallowed and then slowly began to count. One, two, three, four, five!

David's eyes remained closed.

Sheez! It was going to be one of those days. He counted again and again, and still his eyes stubbornly refused to open.

Okay, let me think this through, David mused aloud,

rehashing the same thought processes he had gone through countless times before. Obviously, he told himself, there are at least two differing explanations of why my eyes won't open. The first is simply that my brain is merely playing games with my consciousness. My brain *knows* it can open my eyes whenever it wants to, but it just prefers to play around. Ah, but the other possibility is infinitely more interesting. The other possibility is that the *time is not right* for these blue orbs of mine to open up. And if, by some miracle—some sheer force of will—I were able to *defy* the precise clockwork of the entire universe and open my eyes before destiny's timetable, who knows what kind of catastrophe would result? So, I'll just lie here patiently, and when the proper time arrives—

The door to David's room suddenly burst open, and a curiously decorated pillow whizzed through the air as fast as a basketball, aimed straight for his head. It connected with a beautifully satisfying thud, and David's eyes opened. (In reality, his eyes had opened at the sound of the door bursting open, but the ensuing business with the pillow had all happened so quickly it seemed to David that the pillow's encounter with his head was the provoking stimulus.)

"You *bastard*, Josh!" he shouted with a laugh, using the word solely in its humorous connotation, a possibility warily agreed to by his father after a prolonged discussion about the matter on the evening before his death. "You bastard tool of destiny!"

"Josh is *not* a bastard, David," his mother's muffled voice called out from another part of the small and somewhat cluttered house. "And I resent the implication immensely."

David rolled over and picked up the pillow, which had fallen to the floor after crashing into his face. The words *Happy* and *Birthday* were printed haphazardly all over the white pillowcase with red and blue marker pens.

David reached for his clothes. "Hey, Mom! You should see what Joshy did! Boy, is *he* in trouble. He wrote all over one of your *good* pillowcases, Mom. Oh, no! I think it's one of those *old* ones of Grandma's, with all that pretty embroidery and stuff. Let's see here, let me just test this—Yep! Just as I feared! It's *permanent*, Mom! He wrote all over it with *permanent* marker pens. Boy, are you going to be mad! I think you'll probably want to ground him for a month when you see—"

David, dressed now—except for his shoes—stood

against his wall with the pillow poised in his upraised hands. Just as he expected, his ten-year-old brother reappeared in the doorway, wide-eyed and hesitant. David took aim, then whammo! "Gotcha, Joshpot! Right in the kisser!"

"What's a tool of destiny, anyway?" Josh asked, dropping a Junkpuff into the toaster.

"Mom, I need you to sign something," David said, tapping his pen on a piece of binder paper on which he had just finished writing.

"Okay, dear. Just a second." His mother was rummaging around in the refrigerator. "Oh, no! We're not out of half-and-half again, are we?" She shut the refrigerator door and stepped over to where David was sitting. "Happy birthday, Davey," she said quietly, kissing the top of his head. "We'll celebrate tonight, okay?"

"Sure, Mom. That's fine." David felt a sudden thickness in his throat. He knew she was thinking of his father, and missing him. It was always worse on birthdays and holidays for him, too. He glanced up at his mother and quickly looked away. He felt his eyes begin to sting.

"Oh boy!" Josh exclaimed suddenly. "Can we have chocolate cake and bubble-gum ice cream, maybe? No, wait! I got it! Let's go to Fenton's! I want a banana split, that huge one they—"

"Hey, hold it, buster! Whose B-day is it, anyway?" David asked, pretending to be indignant, but grateful to his brother for unwittingly helping to direct his thoughts away from the sadness of the past.

Josh treated David to one of his more hideous faces before starting to blow on his steaming tart. "Mom," he whined, "David called me a bastard tool of destiny and he won't tell me what it means. Make him tell me what it means, okay, Mom?"

"What flavor is that thing?" David asked. "Is that the *last* Redstuff Junkpuff you're eating? Are you finishing the *last* of the red ones?"

Josh hunched over his breakfast, protecting it with cupped hands. "Well, there's a whole *box* of Yellowstuff ones, *Da*-vid!"

"Yellowstuff! Bah! Only yuckies eat Yellowstuff Junkpuffs."

"Well, *you* were eating one yesterday, stupid! So you must be a yucky, right?"

David's mother had just refilled the sugar bowl and was placing it back on the table. Her expression was a mixture of amusement and exasperation. "That's enough, David. Now stop teasing your brother. You called him something, and he has a right to know what it means."

David hung his head in exaggerated penance. "Oh, all right, Josh," he said. "I'll try to explain it to you. A tool of destiny is just another way of saying you are a contrivance of predeterminism, an instrument of fate, a chip off the old block of chance, a—"

"Mom, make him explain it *right*, okay?"

"But don't you want to know what a bastard is, Josh?" David asked innocently. "I called you a bastard, too, didn't I?"

"Well, I already *know* what a bastard is! So I don't need a big old stupid bastard like you to tell me what a bastard is, do I?"

David burst out laughing before he could stop himself, while Josh smiled and turned his head, pleased with his sudden and unexpected victory.

"So what is this thing?" the boys' mother asked, leaning over David's shoulder, coffee cup in hand. She quickly read the short paragraph. "What *is* this? Are you serious about it, David?" she asked, picking up the sheet of paper.

He nodded, so she read it again, aloud this time. " 'To Mr. Frazier: My son, David Bruce Schumacher, has my permission to change his name to The Blue Avenger. It is my understanding that the only requirement for a name change in this state is simply to start using the new moniker, so, in your capacity as David's school counselor, will you please make the necessary corrections on your state-of-the-art computerized records. All best wishes, Sally Schumacher.' "

David's mom straightened up, sighed, and crossed her arms. "I'm not going to sign that, David. I can't sign that."

David swallowed. Actually, it was more of a gulp. He really hadn't anticipated a problem with this. He thought he knew his mother. They had an understanding. They had discussed things thoroughly during a marathon session shortly after his father's death, and—up to now—they had enjoyed a textbook perfect mother-son relationship. They had hammered out their priorities; some things were important and some things were not. He was to have complete freedom as long as his actions were not deemed detrimental to his and/or others' physical or mental health. It was the kind of a bargain that would work only if made with a decent kid—and, fortunately, that is what David Bruce Schumacher was—formed out of Sally Schumacher's perfect April egg and Walter J. Schumacher's spermatozoon number 14,889,004. So now, what was all this, then? He had kept his end of the bargain. Surely changing his name would not be detrimental to—

"I will not use a word like *moniker* in this sort of document," his mother declared, tapping the paper with the back of her hand.

David let out his breath in a long, low whistle. "Whew. You had me worried there for a minute, Mom."

He ripped out the page from his binder and hastily wrote out a new one. "There," he said. "It's changed."

Josh, who had been sitting at the table in rapt attention, finally spoke. "The Blue Avenger? I'm going to be the brother of The Blue Avenger? Like that stupid cartoon character you draw? Oh, come *on!* Give me a break!"

"Stand proud, bro' Josh! Stand proud!"

"So what's your *first* name going to be, for God's

sake—*The?* Is your first name *The?* How original! Spelled *b-o-r-i-n-g!*"

David raised his head slightly and held it perfectly still, like an animal in the forest listening to sounds of impending danger. Finally he spoke. "You know, the tool is right! By Jove, Josh, you're absolutely right!"

He tore out the page and crumpled it up. "But how can I—? Oh, the problem, the *problem!* What to do about the *The!*" He buried his head in his hands, running his fingers through his thick red curls and along the sides of his thin, freckled, and sunburned face.

And then in a flash it came to him. "Of course! I've got it! It's so simple!" He suddenly stood up on his chair and raised his arms dramatically toward the ceiling. "Mom, Josh—behold your son and brother! Secret champion of the underdog, modest seeker of truth, fearless innovator of the unknown. A comic-strip character come to life! Forget the *The!* It's simply Blue Avenger, at your service!"

"Blue," his mother said, "get down off the chair, will you? And you two better get moving. You'll be late for school."

★ ★ ★

David had one small task to perform before he could leave for school that morning: He needed to decide on a word, for it was his turn to "bringaword" to his English class that day.

"Bringaword" and "bringaquote" were two of Ms. Chandler's ideas. The last five minutes of every English period were devoted to discussing the day's word or quotation, which the students took turns contributing. David invariably brought words of a philosophical nature; words such as *determinism* and *hylozoism* were typical of his contributions. On his previous turn (twenty-nine school days before), after the five-minute discussion of his word *determinism*, Ms. Chandler asked the class for hands. The doctrine that "everything, including one's choice of action, is the necessary result of a sequence of causes" was voted down by a decisive twenty-eight-to-one sweep, with one abstention.

By all rights that should have settled the matter, but Omaha Nebraska Brown, a new girl this semester and the one "no" vote (David being the abstainer), gave the idea another chance a few days later when her turn came up by contributing *free will*—freedom of decision or of choice between alternatives—which was allowed by Ms.

Chandler even though it was, technically speaking, *two* words. The old reversal ruse fooled no one, however, and the vote on that occasion was the same, with twenty-eight to one in *favor* of the idea (David again abstaining). The results of the vote only confirmed the obvious: Human beings desperately *want* to believe that they are in charge of their own destinies, and it will be a cold day in *#%! before anyone can convince them otherwise.

Finite: adj.: having measurable or definable limits; not infinite. That's a good one, David thought, slamming shut the dictionary. (He would continue to think of himself as "David" until that afternoon, when he would officially notify his school counselor of the change.) Then he grabbed up his books, called out a "So long, Mom," and hurried through the door.

David's house is similar to most of the others on his block—small and boxlike, with a stucco exterior and a thin, shingled roof. There are large cracks in the cement steps leading to the porchless front doors, and peeling paint is the rule rather than the exception. The tiny rectangle patches of front yards are overgrown with the spindly umbrella-like seedpods of Bermuda grass, although an occasional house boasts a neglected rose-bush or, perhaps, a smattering of purple iris.

It usually takes David five and one-half minutes to walk the seven blocks from his house to San Pablo Avenue, from where it is a straight ten-minute shot to school. The problem area is San Pablo Park, a bleak zone of weeds and bushes and stumpy trees, and home to a growing number of scruffy and nondescript *Homo sapiens* specimens, who always ask David for "some change" or "a cig" as he passes them on his way to school. Well, David doesn't smoke, but he does have change in his pocket and is therefore made edgy and uncomfortable by this almost constant mooching.

So on this January morning, the morning of his sixteenth birthday, David decided to quicken his pace and take the long route to school, circling around in back of the park and avoiding any possible confrontation. As he walked along, he began to think about his word, *finite*, and its opposite, *infinite*. The number of grains of sand on all the beaches of the world? he asked himself. Finite or infinite? Finite, of course, he quickly decided. Impossible to count, practically speaking, but finite nevertheless. So what objects on earth could rightly be called infinite? He looked at the ground. Blades of grass? No. Too numerous to count, but still with definable limits. But wait. What about numbers themselves? Numbers. They go on and on, infinitely—

"Hey, Schumacher! Wait up!"

David turned around, recognizing the voice. It was Mike Fennell, his friend since kindergarten, a kid whose severe and basic shyness only David and two other guys at school had managed to penetrate. (Actually, there had been three, but the third one had moved away with his family after the earthquake that had collapsed the Oakland freeway and devastated the San Francisco Marina.)

David kept walking but backward, and more slowly. He smiled inwardly, anticipating Mike's question—the usual, *So hey, what's up?*

Mike was breathing hard after his sprint to catch up. "So hey, what's up?" he asked. Not one person in existence knew or even suspected that Mike Fennell had come as close as one could to putting a bullet through his head at twelve minutes after ten o'clock the night before.

David shot a quick glance at his friend's face, splotched with angry red welts the size of giant peas, and felt the same familiar gut-tightening pang of pain and sympathy that the sight always aroused in him. He hesitated a moment before replying. "Oh," he said, looking up at the sky, "I'm just walking along to school on this crisp, sunny morning, humming a tune and thinking about Mary Ann Olson's bazooms."

Mike clenched his teeth and gripped David's arm. "Oh, you slimeball!" He started to squeeze, easy at first, and then harder and harder. "Take that back, you—you *#%! toadie!"

"Okay! Okay! Release me!" David laughed. "I really wasn't thinking about her boobies at all. I was thinking about her—"

"Just stop right there!" Mike suddenly hooked his arm around David's neck in a death-lock grip. "Say uncle, you *#%!, or you die."

"Uncle! Uncle!" David gurgled, flapping his arms around wildly.

"All right, then." Mike let him go after a final, just-for-good-measure wrench, and they walked the rest of the way to school in peace, kicking up the junk that was strewn along the edges of the sidewalk—the Coke cans and crumpled cigarette packs and paper cups from Burger King, with their clear plastic lids and protruding straws still attached. At one point along the route, David couldn't help smiling; Mike Fennell was the only guy he knew who would say a thing like "Say uncle, you *#%!, or you die."

The number of events that had also occurred at four minutes and thirty-five seconds before seven that morning—at the exact time that David had decided to change his name—could be correctly termed *finite*, but oh, what an astronomical number that would be! Here are just seven of them, all but one of which would eventually turn out to affect David's life—to a smaller or larger degree:

○ An unusually large terrestrial isopod (commonly known as a sow bug—genus *Oniscus*, for the scientific minded) was seriously injured when it was run over by a power lawn mower driven by a city schools employee as the machine rounded the wide turn near the old barracks classrooms at San Pablo High School, located at the corner of San Pablo Avenue and Jackson Street, somewhere in the vast gray suburbs of Oakland, California, U.S.A., Earth, Universe, Unknown.

○ A Wonder Bread delivery truck driver, also speeding along San Pablo Avenue close to where it joined the freeway, swerved to avoid hitting a large foam sofa cushion that had fallen off an open U-Haul trailer moments before, and, in swerving, ran over a brown paper bag full of kitchen garbage that had been tossed out of a recreational vehicle during the night, smashing it to smithereens and projecting the empty outer package of a small (three-ounce-size) orange Jell-O brand dessert mix into an adjacent strip of weeds, where it lodged itself against the chain-link fence adjoining the spacious tree-lined parking lot of the new seven-story Benevolent Trust Altruistic Five-Way Insurance Company, Inc.

○ A swarm of newly arrived "killer bees" from the southern part of town had just settled into a temporary home under the overhanging ledge of the gymnasium at San Pablo High School and would soon begin to send forth their honey scouts, followed by scores of gung ho workers— a glorious feat of nature that would occur that very afternoon during a short presentation of awards to the San Pablo High boys' tennis team, which had placed third in the league last season.

○ Annie Marzipan, America's most beloved and admired newspaper columnist and late-night television guest ("Ask Auntie Annie"), living on the east coast of the United States—where, due to the time differential, it was four minutes and thirty-five seconds before *ten* in the morning—cut into the lemon meringue pie she had painstakingly made the night before for important luncheon guests (the president of the board of a large cornstarch company among them) and was dismayed to see it collapse in a disgusting, drippy, semiliquid runny mess.

○ Deep within the tectonic plates of the earth's crust, beneath the ocean floor in the waters adjacent to the city of Los Angeles (in one of the long-dormant and previously unrecognized "hidden faults" involved in the formation of the transverse ranges of southern California), a barely perceptible tremor caused a small fissure (the proverbial last straw), which would be responsible for pinpointing the exact location of the raising to the surface of a new island (surprising the bejabbers out of the earthquake experts at the U.S. Geological Survey) the approximate size of seven football fields—just half a mile from shore—during a major earthquake at sea that was scheduled to occur by the forces that be in exactly eleven years and three days and that would level the luxurious beach high-rise called La-La Land, killing the 459 men, women, and children living there, three of whom would have died that day anyway from various other causes.

○ Mrs. Fran Manning, the principal of San Pablo High School, was toweling off her hair after shampooing with a popular new brand of conditioning shampoo called Honey-Doo, made with "pure, all natural honey," as well as (according to the label) fifteen other ingredients, including Ergocalciferol, Stearamidopropyl dimethylamine, and Methylchloroisothiazolinone.

○ A significant chemical change (involving a

buildup of beta-amyloid protein fragments, implicated in Alzheimer's disease) occurred in the brain of a Mrs. Laverne Livingstone, a retired high school principal presently residing in a nursing home just outside of Austin, Texas.

two

Omaha Nebraska Brown is an unusual name for a girl, but that's what happens sometimes. Her mother just liked the sound of it, and her father had no objections. Her father's name is Mr. Johnny Brown, and her mother's name is Margie. Johnny, Margie, and Omaha all used to live together in Tulsa, Oklahoma, until everything went kerflooey.

Johnny Brown is a member of that small but puzzling brotherhood of men—all of a certain age—who teeter on the fringe of the so-called American Dream, always on the outside, looking in—like everyone's cousin Eric, or Craig, that quiet, thin-haired man down the block who lives at home with his widowed mother and walks alone to the bakery every Sunday morning for a newspaper and a chocolate éclair. Some die-hard affiliates of Johnny's brotherhood are still out in Arizona making geodesic domes; others are part-time night-shift stock shelvers at Safeway or Lucky's; but most just drift from job to job, spending their free time drinking coffee with lots of sugar and reading paperback books at sidewalk cafés adjacent to colleges. When they happen to run into each other, they laugh and say they can't remember when they had their last joint, and many of them are telling the truth. "The war—that's what did it," folks say now with sympathetic nods, and that assessment is partly true. Those young men who opposed the war in Vietnam on religious grounds—the so-called conscientious objectors—were allowed to accept alternate public service assignments at home. Other protesters fled across the border to Canada, while a small number just faced the music and served their time in jail. That was the path that Johnny took. It was the bravest thing he'd ever done, facing the angry, flag-waving crowds, standing up for what he felt was right. It changed him, defined him, and made him what he is today.

When he was finally released from jail, a friend helped him land a job in the Tulsa General Hospital as an orderly, and that's where he met Margie quite by accident late one Thursday night. As it happened, a Mrs. Purdy in room 412 became actively nauseated without a receptacle, and the call went forth for both an orderly and a nurse's aide. Johnny proceeded to mop up the floor while Margie mopped up Mrs. Purdy. (Neither Johnny nor Margie have ever consciously acknowledged that they were brought together because Mrs. Purdy puked.)

At the time, Margie was an unmarried mother of an eight-year-old holy terror named Travis, and she was several years older than Johnny—a fact that didn't seem to bother him in the least. Johnny and Margie had gone to thirty-two movies together, shared sixteen fast-food lunches, enjoyed fifty-four sit-down dinners, ordered fifteen Chinese takeouts, and risked twenty-two sleepovers before Margie got preggers with Omaha Nebraska, and after that they lived together as man and wife for eleven years and 287 days. Johnny, like most of the other men in his brotherhood, was afraid of marriage or commitments of any kind, but at least he was willing to go along with Margie's suggestion that they could *pretend* they were married for baby Omaha's sake, and he did agree to let the little bundle take his name. Margie felt certain that she would be able to talk him into making it legal sooner or later, but whenever she broached the subject, he would play the same old record—the tune about a marriage license being "only a piece of paper." After much work and perseverance (made even more difficult by the existence of Travis and little Omaha) Margie became a registered nurse, and although Johnny was only three college credits short of earning a degree in philosophy, he never got around to writing the final term paper that was required. In the meantime, he was content to work in the classified advertising department of the *Suburban Shopping News.* The *SSN,* as it is called, is thrown on front sidewalks, lawns, driveways, or roofs of 30,444 residences in the greater Tulsa area every Wednesday afternoon, where it lies around for several days before being tossed into the nearest garbage can or trash pile, accompanied by phrases like "Oh, this stupid paper again!" and "What a nuisance!" and, from the truly perplexed, "There should be a law against scattering this *#%! all over the neighborhood!"

The war may be partly to blame for that group of non-conforming dropout males like Johnny, but many suspect the real culprit was the glue, the glue and the "dope" (oh, so aptly named!) that the boys required in order to construct their model airplanes in those bygone days.

They used the glue to join the delicate balsa wood pieces (after they had pinned them ever so carefully, following the thin blue lines indicated on their wax-paper-covered plans), and then they papered over their fuselage, wing, and tail assembly frameworks and used the "dope" like paint to seal the flimsy tissue and make it strong. "You kids get out of that basement now and get some fresh air!" their mothers used to holler down the stairs. Hours later the boys would emerge, dizzy and glassy-eyed, the toluene of the glue and dope playing havoc with their brains. (This sad phenomenon has yet to be verified by definitive studies at prestigious universities, but the mothers know. The mothers and the sisters, who were excluded from the cellars and are therefore normal, remember the glue and the dope, and they know.)

When Omaha Nebraska Brown was a dark-haired, serious-eyed eleven-year-old in Tulsa, Oklahoma, the new office manager of the *Suburban Shopping News,* where her father worked, inexplicably instituted a dress code for the men that banned beards and required neckties. Well, that was it for Mr. Johnny Brown. That double whammy, combined with the fact that he and Margie had grown sick to death of each other, just sent him reeling over the edge. The commonly used expression would be that "something snapped in his brain," but that phrase, while vivid and imaginative, is never meant to be taken literally. The fact is that nobody knows for sure what happened in Omaha's father's brain, only that he came home from work that day, packed two suitcases—mostly with his books—hugged Omaha in an embrace that almost smothered her, saluted Margie in an oddly cold and aloof fashion, and walked away from the house in long strides, the tears rolling down into his beard like raindrops in a summer storm.

Omaha would never forget what he said to her before he left, partly because his leaving was such a traumatic experience for her, but more than that because of the terrible image his words produced in her exceptionally bright and retentive young mind. "I have to go now, baby," he said, "and I know I'll never see you again. And because your mama's so mad at me" (and here he tried to playfully tweak her nose, even though his face was contorted with pain) "sure as shootin' she's going to move away with you and never leave a forwarding address. I myself am going to pursue my lifelong dream at last, which is to research and write a book about a very heroic and tragic man from long ago—a man who had the guts to stand up for what he believed, and even though they tied him to a stake and burned him alive in the public square, he refused to recant. I'll always love you, and I'm sorry it has to be this way. Take care of yourself, and keep the peace." (Only 11 percent of the men in Johnny's "club" still say "keep the peace," at least occasionally, and more than half of them would admit to feeling self-conscious about it, as if they were using passé slang, like "hippie" or "dig it.")

Omaha would remember Johnny's words so well that she would be able to repeat them almost verbatim to David Bruce Schumacher exactly five years and thirty-seven days later in Oakland, California, when the desire to find her father—which had been building and building throughout the years—would finally surface like a diver emerging from the deep, bursting forth above the water with a shout and outstretched arms.

It is not surprising that Omaha couldn't sleep the night her father left. She crawled out of bed when the clock struck midnight and made her way to the kitchen. Her mother was sitting at the table with her head in her arms. The evening paper was strewn about, and when Omaha entered the room, the slight change in the air current was enough to send part of the Metro section sliding from the chair to the floor.

"Oh, darling." Margie sighed. "Come here."

As Omaha approached her, Margie scooped up the fallen newspaper. "I don't believe this," she murmured. "I just don't believe it. Joyce *Maynard!* Who's *she*, for God's sake? It says he had an affair with Joyce Maynard!"

Omaha wiped her nose with her sleeve and managed to whimper, "He told me he would never see me again, Mom. Why did he say that?"

Margie looked momentarily puzzled. "Oh," she said. "That. Well, honey, it's okay. Your father has just boogied himself right out of our lives, but we'll get along fine. Just don't you worry about that."

Omaha was only eleven, but she was hip and knew all about the other-woman syndrome. "Who's Joyce Maynard?" she asked fearfully, wanting to know yet not wanting to know, because she was eleven years old and had always loved her quiet but slightly off-center daddy.

Margie pointed to the paper. What a state she was in. "Here! Look! It says she had an affair with J. D. Salinger! He was fifty-three at the time and she was only twenty! I just can't *believe* that! He never even *answered* my letters, the bum! After I read *The Catcher in the Rye*, I wrote to him dozens of times! And besides, he was supposed to be a *recluse*, for God's sake!"

Omaha Nebraska couldn't believe her ears. Her mother didn't even *care* that Johnny Brown was gone forever. But that's what happens when love flies out the window.

Three weeks after Johnny Brown had split, Margie's holy terror son (and Omaha's half brother) got himself in very serious trouble. It had been brewing for years. In fact, Margie had thrown in the towel as far as Travis was concerned as soon as he hit fifteen. He was just incorrigible. She couldn't do a thing with him, and neither could Johnny, so even though they still allowed him to live at home, they closed their eyes and shrugged and just let him run wild. So now there he was, twenty years old and serving an eleven-year sentence for killing a drinking buddy with another friend's gun in a rowdy argument over something he could never quite remember.

Before Margie and Omaha left Tulsa forever for what Margie told the post office was "destination unknown" (but was really Omaha, Nebraska), they stopped by the penitentiary to say good-bye to Travis. Since his father had simply vanished into the mist one day, before he was even born, Margie and Omaha were the only known relatives he had in the world. (*Known* relatives, because how could he possibly know that the officer who was standing guard by the prisoners' entrance that day was the great-great-grandson of his father's great-grandmother's youngest brother? Oh, but if he knew, wow! Wouldn't it give him a laugh, though? *Related to the guard!* he would say. *Outasight!* As for the guard, it would really spoil his day. But no matter; neither one would ever find out.)

"I thought I'd better tell you, Travis, we're moving to Omaha, Nebraska," Margie told him while Omaha Nebraska was in the rest room. Even though Travis was her son, she never really liked him much. In the back of her mind—so far back she wasn't even conscious of it—she had always hoped to have a son like Harry

McGinnis, the easygoing curly-headed little Irish kid who sat beside her in kindergarten and could already read the first graders' books. But Travis was nothing like Harry McGinnis. Travis was like his father—angular, blond, hotheaded, and dyslexic.

"I have a job waiting for me in Omaha," Margie said flatly, not even bothering to explain to him that she had always loved the name of that town. "The thing is, I'm trying to ditch Johnny Brown once and for all. And listen, Travis. If by some fluky chance he finds out you're in here and comes around asking for us, will you please do me a huge favor and tell him you don't know where we went? I never want to see him again." (Margie could very well have added, "And I never want to see *you* again, either!" but she didn't.)

Travis looked her in the eye. Even though she was his mother, he never really liked her much, and if the truth be known, he often wished she'd just get off his back. Sometimes, out of guilt, she used to pat his hand or try to give him an awkward hug when he was little, but it would always make him feel creepy. Finally he just came out and told her he didn't want her hugging him anymore, and she said that was fine with her.

"Okay," he said, in answer to her request. "I will." He paused and knit his brow. "I mean," he corrected, "I won't." He closed his eyes and sighed. "I sure wish *I* could go to Omaha, Nebraska." He jerked his head around and slapped his thigh. "Dang!" he said. Only he didn't say "dang." What he really said was *#%!.

To know all is to forgive all, as the sweet maxim goes. Were Margie's actions regarding Johnny Brown and her son, Travis, mean and vindictive? Well, some might say that. But oh, can anyone really know the *depth* of the resentment and pain the two had caused her throughout the years? Why couldn't Travis behave like a regular kid? Why was he always in trouble? And then there was Johnny. Why couldn't he have just gone ahead and *married* her, for God's sake? After all, it's only a piece of paper!

Omaha could barely stand to say good-bye to Travis that day, since she really loved him like a brother. Years before he started getting into trouble, he would amuse her with the most daredevil stunts anyone could ever dream of, like jumping off the highest part of the garage into a pile of leaves, holding an umbrella for a parachute and shouting, "Watch out belooww . . ." as he hurled himself through the air like a giant bird wearing cowboy boots. When he was twelve and she was three, he broke his ankle after sliding down the chimney and landing kerplunk in the fireplace after trying to prove to her that Santa Claus could really pull it off. He was still ho-ho-hoing even as he was being carried into the emergency room on a stretcher, trying to wipe the soot from his arms but succeeding only in spreading it around all the more.

Now, at the jail, sitting in the crowded visitors' room at the brown Formica tables, the two of them were laughing, recalling those incidents of former days but being careful not to mention those other times—those occasional uncontrolled fits of anger that would some-times overtake poor Travis, brought on by who knows what, and finally leaving him sobbing and bitter with grief at the pain he had caused.

When their visiting time was up and Margie and Omaha were walking toward the visitors' exit, Travis's unknown relative watched unmoved as Omaha broke away and ran back for one last tearful good-bye. "Trav!

Trav!" she shouted, just as he was about to go back into the prisoners' quarters. "I'll—I'll—" She almost started to say that she would write to him, until she remembered he could barely read. So instead she cried, "I'll come and see you again, Trav! I promise I will! When I'm grown up, I will!"

Travis turned and smiled, and gave her the thumbs-up sign made famous by pilots wearing goggles and leather helmets in Hollywood war movies. Fifteen days later, for reasons known only to prison officials, Travis was packed up and transported hundreds of miles away to the Washington State Penitentiary in Walla Walla, Washington, a city famous the world over for its sweet red onions.

And, yes, another unanswered question: If the cause of occasional uncontrolled fits of anger is unknown, does that mean they don't have a cause?

three

On the night before David Schumacher's sixteenth birthday, Omaha Nebraska Brown had a dream about her father. She kept calling to him in a strange, echoey voice, but all she could see of him was a flash of his brown corduroy pant leg as he kept disappearing around the curvy bends of hedges or the sharp-angled corners of redbrick buildings. It wasn't that she was an unhappy girl; it was just that she felt cheated—out of both a brother *and* a father.

After she and Margie had moved to Omaha, she was obliged to spend every afternoon after school and her entire summers in the public library, since the librarians didn't charge a cent for kid-sitting, and Margie had to work. So when Ms. Anderson, her seventh-grade English-history core teacher, assigned a "scrapbook of newspaper articles that interest you," Omaha had plenty of time to comply. She began saving news stories that dealt with the subject of heredity and environment and what role each plays in the way people react to the events in their lives—a scrapbook for which she is still collecting articles even to this day. (While Ms. Anderson thought it was an interesting topic, she gave Omaha only a C, however, mostly because of the meager number of articles on that subject. On the other hand, Jeffrey Acres garnered an A, since his subject was "Disasters," and his scrapbook was the fattest in the class.)

Like Blue, Omaha had become obsessed with the question of "free will versus fate" at an early age, not realizing, of course, the profundity of the philosophical question with which she was grappling. All Omaha was interested in was innocence and guilt. If choices are impossible, she reasoned, how can there then be guilt? Was it *really* Travis's fault that he lost control and did such a terrible deed? Was there *any* way he could have stopped himself? And if so, why *didn't* he? And what about her father? What could be so *terrible* about wearing a tie to work and shaving off his beard? How *could* he just walk out on them, knowing he would never see his family again? Could it be that he just couldn't help it?

The very first article in Omaha's scrapbook was about identical twins who had been separated at birth. This is the headline and a very short synopsis:

NATURE VS. NURTURE
Genes, Not Environment,
May Shape Personality

The point of this article was that it now appears that our genes play a much larger role in human behavior than was formerly realized. Characteristics such as alcoholism, anxiety, criminality, intelligence, political attitudes, religion, sociability, vocational interests, and more are all related to the genes we inherit from our parents. Of special interest to Omaha, of course, was the inclusion of the word *criminality*.

Her second article was about something called emotional intensity:

HIGHS AND LOWS OF PERSONALITIES
The Excitable vs. the Placid
Emotional Intensity Can Vary Greatly

According to this article, people born with high emotional intensity (which, the story said, was "largely hereditary, showing up virtually from birth and persisting throughout life") naturally tended to react much more strongly to everything than those born with low emotional intensity. Omaha thought that was a most interesting article indeed.

Margie had been right, though, that night in Tulsa so long ago when she had assured Omaha that they would be just fine, because they were, even after they left Omaha, Nebraska, behind and journeyed to Oakland, California, in response to a wonderful career opportunity for Margie—as she had been recommended for and hired as the supervising nurse in a newly formed intensive-care unit for drug-addicted newborn babies. It was a bad situation for the babies, but a good one for Margie.

If a survey had been taken among all the boys at San Pablo High regarding Omaha's looks, it would have disclosed the following information: 87.32 percent would have marked her "average looking," 3.33 percent would call her "below average," 7.67 percent would rate her "above average," and 1.68 percent would think she was "absolutely beautiful." For reasons that harked back partly to the dawn of time and partly to their early imprinting, the 1.68 percent who thought her beautiful would be attracted to her slightly protruding upper jaw, wide mouth, and small, deeply set eyes.

Although her usual expression was mild and pleasing, Omaha rarely smiled. But when she did, it was as real as rain. And the same could be said of her laugh, since her sense of humor was both subtle and discriminating. Her gaze was steady, and she stood as straight as the reeds that sprang up in the marshlands near the bay. She loved to swim, and she could be found nearly every weekend doing leisurely laps at the Y. Her clean, smooth strokes caused hardly a ripple in the water, and her glides were as sleek and swift as an arrow. Observers sometimes remarked that she "swam like an Indian" or "an Indian princess." And indeed (although she didn't know it), she *had* a streak of Cherokee blood in her veins inherited from her mother, the same as Travis, her half brother, the convicted felon, still incarcerated in the Washington State Penitentiary in Walla Walla for his part in the death of a belligerent buddy in a drunken rage over—yes, over what? When the fight was done, neither man could remember. (But then, of course, one of them was dead.)

Omaha never spoke of Travis, but she thought of him often. Although she knew what he had done was wrong, she also knew in her bones that Travis could no more have stopped himself from the violence he had committed that night in the bar than a month-old baby in its crib could stop its insistent cries caused by thirst or hunger or the uncomfortable feeling of wetness around its soft little bottom.

It was fifth period at San Pablo High School on the sixteenth anniversary of David Schumacher's birth, and he was standing at the front desk in the guidance counselor's office. He had purposely waited until fifth period to do the required paperwork because he knew that was the period Omaha worked in the office as a student assistant, and somehow he wanted her to be the first to know. (Had David been asked to participate in the survey regarding Omaha's looks, he would have been included in the 1.68 percent who thought she was absolutely beautiful.)

"Oh, hello, Omaha," David said, pretending he was surprised to see her. He had no sooner spoken those words than the thought flashed through his mind like a turned-on lightbulb in a comic strip—*When my name is Blue Avenger, I will never pretend again!*

"I stopped by here at noon," he said, drumming his fingers nervously on the counter, "and they told me I could see Mr. Frazier anytime this period without an appointment." He glanced toward the back of the room, where his counselor was ensconced in his small, glassed-in cubicle. "Uh, is there a phone book here I could look at before I go in?"

Omaha reached her hands behind her head and swooped her long dark hair up into a ponytail for just an instant before releasing it. "Sure," she said. "White or yellow?"

"White, please."

She reached under the counter. "Here you go."

"Thanks." David quickly flipped through the front pages, past the section on Nuclear Emergency Information and the Earthquake Survival Guide, right to the *A* listings. He ran his finger down the columns. "Hey, great!" he said. "No Avengers."

"Pardon me?"

"I was just checking. There's no Avengers. I'll be the first. When I get my own phone, that is."

"What are you talking about, David?"

Her directness was one of the things he liked best about her. There was no fooling around with Omaha. "I'm about to change my name to Blue Avenger," he said, very clearly and distinctly so that she wouldn't have to ask *What?* "That's why I'm here to see Mr. Frazier." He paused, four beats. "So what do you think of that?"

She paused, too. A perfect beat and a half. "Well, I think it's weird. But how do you do that, anyway? How do you go about changing your name?"

"I heard on a talk show a couple of nights ago that the easiest way to do it is just to start using the new name. This lawyer said you can also do it officially, through the courts and all that, but it's not necessary. Just start using it. That's all you need to do."

"Really? Hmm." She did that thing with her hair again. She didn't mean to be sexy or provocative; it was just a habit with her. Then she murmured, "Blue, huh? Blue. Well, that's nice. I like it. But your last name—Avenger—did you say? I'm not so sure about that. It sounds a little threatening to me. Unless you're a rock band, of course. You're not, are you? You're not the leader of a rock band by any chance?"

"Nope. I don't play an instrument, and I don't even like rock music—not all that much, at least. I guess there's something wrong with me."

"Obviously so," she agreed. "Well, then, have you considered something like Blue Moon or Blue Lagoon instead? How about Blue Berry, Blue Blood, Blue Cheese—"

David held up his hand. "All good suggestions, I'm sure, but there is work to be done, wrongs to be righted, important philosophical questions to be answered—jobs that could never be done by a Blue Berry or a Blue Cheese."

The intercom buzzed. "Yes?" said Omaha. "No, Mr. Frazier. He hasn't called back. But David Schumacher is here." She paused. "Okay, I'll send him in." Omaha touched David's arm. "Go get 'em, Blue," she said, and David knew his life would never be the same.

"You want to do *what?*" Mr. Frazier asked, snatching the sheet of binder paper from David's hand.

"Just change my name, that's all. My mother signed for me. See? She—"

"*#%!, David!" Mr. Frazier loosened his tie even more than it was already, grimacing and twisting his neck around as if he were hanging from a noose. "Excuse my French," he said, lowering his voice and glancing out the door of his cubicle, since he had recently been reprimanded again about his "inappropriate language" by

Mrs. Manning, the principal. "But I can't be bothered with something like this now! I'm expecting a call from—" The phone on Mr. Frazier's desk rang, and he snatched it off the hook like a hot potato. "Yes?" He paused, then exhaled slowly. "Yes, Viola. Who is it now?" He reached for a pencil and a pad of paper. "Stephanie who? Oh, yeah. Stephanie Marshall." He quickly jotted down the name. "So when's she due? Okay. Well, no. I'm not surprised. Thanks."

Mr. Frazier hung up the phone and then folded his arms and stared at David for several seconds. "Gang fights, pregnant girls, and now a screwball kid who wants to change his name. I've been a counselor for thirteen years, and this is the first time I ever got such a dumb, numskull request as this. Why the *#%! do you want to change your name, David? Two weeks from now you'll just want to change it back again." Mr. Frazier quickly read over the sheet of binder paper once more. "Blue Avenger? What's that supposed to mean, for God's sake? Now get out of here and don't bother me about this anymore. I've got work to do."

David Bruce Schumacher (Blue Avenger) didn't move a muscle.

"Good-bye, David!"

"All you have to do is punch it into the computer, Mr. Frazier. It's no big deal. Just find *Schumacher, David,* and punch it out. Then punch in *Avenger, Blue.* That's all there is to it. That's the beauty of computers. No fuss, no muss, no crasers—"

No one spoke for exactly ninety-four seconds. (That's not a very long time in the big scheme of things, but in this situation, it seemed to both participants like a *very* long time.) Finally Mr. Frazier stood up and walked over to the computer—the one hooked into the central office. Then he glanced at David. "For your information, son, it's a lot more complicated than just punching out and punching in." He sat down at the console. "But what the *#%!. If you want to be Blue Avenger, who am I to stop you? Now there goes the bell. Get out of here before I throw you out."

"Thanks, Mr. Frazier," Blue Avenger said, in a voice like molten steel. "And if there's anything I can ever do for you, just let me know."

Mr. Frazier stood up to escort the young man out of his cubicle. My God, he thought suddenly. Am I seeing things, or has this kid just grown six inches?

★ ★ ★

Omaha was waiting for Blue outside the counselor's office, which pleased him no end but did not surprise him in the least.

"It's official, then?" she asked, looking up at him. "Your name is now Blue Avenger?"

"Yes," he said. "It's official. And thank you for waiting for me. Don't you have a class out by the barracks next period?"

"Yes, I do. And you do, too, if I'm not mistaken."

"You're not mistaken," he said, and together they left the building and started walking down the concrete pathway toward the barracks classrooms. It was an unseasonably warm afternoon for January, and there was no breeze at all. Blue noticed the moisture in fine little beads on Omaha's forehead and neck, and it almost made him swoon with pleasure. Suddenly she stopped walking and stooped down to examine something on the edge of the sidewalk. She slid her book bag off her shoulder and reached down to touch whatever it was that had attracted her attention. Blue had gone on several paces without her, but when he saw her absorbed there, he came back to see what was delaying her.

"What is it?" he asked. "It looks like a bug."

Omaha turned her head slightly and looked at him, her smooth dark hair trailing over one shoulder. "It's a sow bug," she said. "And look at the size of him. He's as big as a peanut. He's hurt. Every time he tries to walk, he flips over on his back."

She righted the isopod once more, and sure enough, it immediately flopped over again on its back, the remaining few of its original myriad little legs kicking around in a frenzy.

"The bell's going to ring in a minute," Blue said. "Come on."

"Okay," she said, but she just kept on fingering the sow bug, trying to coax it into walking properly. Blue tapped her on the shoulder then, and she looked up at him with an expression of such compassion and sympathy it almost took his breath away. (He didn't know it then, of course, but through the years, that expression would return again and again in his mind's eye, each time filling him anew with wonder and tenderness.)

Omaha picked up her book bag and stood up. Then, with a strong, swift stamp of her foot, she smashed the sow bug into the sidewalk, leaving nothing but a slightly splintery wet spot about the size of a quarter.

"Yikes!" Blue exclaimed. "Why'd you do *that?*"

She seemed taken aback at his question. "Well, what's better?" she asked impatiently, quickening her pace. "For him to die a slow death baking on his back in the sun all afternoon or to just get stamped into oblivion before he knew what hit him?"

They had almost reached the barracks by now, and their paths were about to part. They stopped walking, and Blue put the back of his hand up to her neck, touching the dampness there. "I love you, Omaha Nebraska Brown," he said, surprising the daylights out of himself. "And Blue Avenger never lies, except in the line of duty."

Omaha was quite surprised herself. She had instinctively known there was something very special about David Bruce Schumacher from the first time she saw him, but she never dreamed he would suddenly blossom out like a hothouse orchid right before her eyes. She honestly couldn't say she loved him, too, however, because she didn't know it yet. But she *did* smile at him in a slightly shy and embarrassed way. And her smiles were always sincere.

four

Even though Mike Fennell's typical modesty had prevented him from telling Blue that he was to receive a plaque for being the "most outstanding sophomore" on last year's tennis team during a little ceremony that afternoon, Blue got wind of it, anyway. The fact is that Mike and the others were supposed to have been honored last June before school let out, but there was some mix-up at the trophy shop and the awards were late—very late—in coming.

So after school, to show support for his friend, Blue meandered over to the courts (which are adjacent to the outdoor swimming pool) to watch the proceedings. Besides the members of the team, Mrs. Manning was there, along with Coach Phelps and a bored junior sports photographer sent over by the local newspaper. All in all, a pretty motley showing. And because of the noise coming from the pool—where swimming practice was about to begin—it was difficult to hear what was being said.

Finally Mrs. Manning climbed up on the green

judges' stand, which was being used as a makeshift stage for the occasion, and reached down to get the box of plaques from one of the team captains. That's when Blue, sitting cross-legged on the court just three feet away from her, first noticed the bees, which were buzzing around in a menacing cloud beneath the over-hanging roof of the gym. One scout, flying far afield and led by the scent of honey, came buzzing around Mrs. Manning's head. She quickly brushed it off her hair as if it were a harmless fly. But the alarm was out. A few seconds later four more bees came flying around angrily, forcing her to quickly duck her head in self-defense.

Several of the more uncouth kids in the crowd started to laugh rudely, but Blue sensed the imminent danger. When he looked up and saw the entire swarm beginning to swerve toward her, he sprang into action. Even though he wasn't wearing his blue fishing vest and matching towel headdress, he acted as if he were. With a quick glance in the direction of the pool, he estimated he could reach it in approximately twenty strides. Leaping up the judges' stand in just two bounds, he swept Mrs. Manning into his arms, ran quickly down the steps (step-step-step-step-step!) like an agile dancer, and raced toward the pool before anyone realized what was happening. (Except, of course, for the sports photographer, who was trained to be always on the alert and who got several excellent shots of the whole thing, including the one that would appear on the first page of the sports section in the morning paper—Blue in a magnificent midair leap into the pool with Mrs. Manning in his arms and a gray cloud of killer bees close behind, about to engulf them both.)

"So what's your name, kid?" the photographer asked as Blue was drying off at the side of the pool and the principal, having thanked him profusely, was headed toward the gym for a change of clothes.

"Blue," Blue replied. "My name is Blue Avenger."

The photographer sighed. Another smart-aleck high school jerk. But if that's the way he wanted to be—

After its appearance on the sports page in the local paper the next morning, the photo was picked up by a major wire service, and the day after that it was seen by millions and millions of people throughout the United States, beneath this headline: BLUE AVENGER TO THE RESCUE! And below it in slightly smaller type: HONEY OF AN IDEA SAVES SCHOOL PRINCIPAL FROM KILLER BEE ATTACK.

A fifty-five-year-old woman in Tampa, Florida, and a man named Steven Stoddard in Los Angeles, California, both phoned their local papers and stopped their subscriptions. They had simply had it up to here with stupid puns in newspaper headlines.

Instant fame—that's what he had. "Yo, Blue!" the kids called out in the hallways. "Way to go!" As he walked into class, someone would announce, "It's Bah-loo Avennnger!" stretching out the name dramatically, as if they were introducing him on some late-night television show.

He was their new hero, and they loved him all the more for the way he accepted their accolades, with just the right blend of genuine humility and humorous bravado. Just for fun, on the second day after his appearance in hundreds of newspapers throughout America, he dressed for school in his father's blue fishing vest with a blue terry cloth towel tied around his head like the Sheik of Araby, and the kids went wild.

Girls who had never given David Schumacher a second look were coming on like gangbusters to Blue Avenger, including a certain blonde named Mary Ann

Olson. This was particularly distressing to him, as this was the same girl with whom his friend Mike was completely and hopelessly obsessed. "Oh, Blue," she said, catching him by the arm after school as he was starting for home. "My dad has a couple of passes to the Warriors game tonight. It starts at eight. Would you like to take me?"

Blue noticed her teeth were tiny and straight and white, just like a shark's. "Actually, Mary Ann," he said, "I can't. I really can't go to the game with you tonight, but I know someone who might."

"Oh, *#%!," she said, pouting. "I wanted to go with you. But who do you have in mind?"

"Well, Mike Fennell really loves the Warriors, and I'm sure—"

"Mike Fennell? The guy with all the zits? Oh, spare me *that*, Blue Avenger!" And she wrinkled up her nose and squished up her mouth.

Blue was disgusted with her and wanted to tell Mike straightaway what a shallow character she really was. But he knew that was something Mike would have to find out for himself. However, he couldn't worry about that at the moment; he had to go home and bake a pie.

★ ★ ★

Like all classical heroes down through the ages, Blue Avenger is not invulnerable; like them, he has a weakness. Superman feared kryptonite, Achilles had his heel. For Blue, it is lemon meringue pie.

Science will one day discover the reason for the extraordinary power that certain foods hold for individual humans. The answer will prove to be much more complicated than expected. It will involve not only the size, shape, and position of certain taste and olfactory receptors but also the interaction of seven specific brain chemicals.

Chocolate, of course, leads the list of temptations, while many persons find it impossible to resist salted peanuts or licorice candy. (There presently lives a woman in Dubuque, Iowa, who simply cannot go to sleep at night without first eating her bowl of shredded wheat with milk and brown sugar, a ritual she has observed every evening without fail for the past forty-seven years.)

Blue could never understand why lemon meringue pie had such a hold over him. All he knew was that he had to have his fix once a week, at the very minimum. And it couldn't be just *any* lemon meringue pie; it had to be homemade, with California Sunkist lemons and fresh ranch eggs.

Blue had been making his own pies for three years, ever since his father died and his mother, a dental hygienist, was obliged to switch from part-time to full-time work. The crust "shell" was a cinch. His mother had guided him through the first few tries, but soon he had mastered the skill. (*Use ice-cold soda instead of water for the crust, and never overhandle the dough,* he would explain cheerfully if asked.) But the chief bugaboo, the bane of his life, was the infernal weeping and dripping of his meringue. Sometimes it bubbled out in tiny droplets on the surface, while other times it slyly hid out of sight, only to run like a river as soon as the first cut was made. Either way, the pie would inevitably collapse on itself with a *sploosh!* and he would be forced to dish it up with a spoon. Luckily the flavor of the pie was not affected, but oh, how he would dearly love to solve the persistent mystery of "weeping meringue"!

It was not that he didn't try. After all, making a meringue simply consisted of beating sugar into egg whites, spreading the mixture over a lemon filling (which he had already prepared and poured into the pie shell), and baking it. How many different ways could there be to do *that*? He consulted every cookbook he could find, and each one had its own "solution" to the problem of weeping meringue. Every time he located a new recipe, he would follow the directions to the letter with his heart in his throat, only to have his hopes cruelly dashed again and again.

Here are some of the suggestions he had found:

○ "Always have the egg whites at *room temperature*. Failure to do this may result in a 'weepy' meringue."

○ "Use fresh eggs *right out of the refrigerator* to prevent a 'weeping' meringue."

○ "*Do not overbeat* the egg whites. Overbeating will cause 'weepy' meringue."

○ "Be sure to beat the sugar into the egg whites until thoroughly dissolved. *Underbeating* will cause the meringue to 'weep.' "

○ "Bake in a *slow oven (300 degrees)* for 20 to 25 minutes so the meringue will dry out and not 'weep.' "

○ "Bake 10 to 15 minutes in a *hot oven (425 degrees)*, and be sure to cool out of drafts to prevent 'weeping.' "

○ "It is very important to spread the meringue to the very edge of the pie. Failure to do this will cause the meringue to shrink and 'weep.' "

After Blue got home from school on the day Mary Ann had invited him to a Warriors game, he found a new meringue recipe staring him in the face right there in the food section of the newspaper. Could this be the one he was waiting for? He couldn't wait to try it. This is how it went: Mix 1 tablespoon cornstarch with 2 tablespoons cold water in a small saucepan. Add ½ cup boiling water and boil (stirring constantly) for 1 minute. Pour into a small bowl and refrigerate for 25 minutes. (Hint: Set the timer.) Then in another bowl beat 3 egg whites and ¼ teaspoon cream of tartar until almost stiff. Slowly add ⅓ cup sugar, still beating. Add the cornstarch mixture all at once and beat until stiff. Spread over the lemon filling and bake at 350 degrees for 15 to 20 minutes or until lightly brown.

Blue made the pie and then the new recipe meringue, following the directions carefully. Although he had to admit that the texture of the meringue was greatly improved, sad to say, it still wept like a baby.

five

The week after Blue's gallant race to the pool with Mrs. Manning in his arms, Mr. Frazier sent the following memo to him in care of his first-period teacher via a student messenger:

> **To:** Blue Avenger
> **From:** Mr. Frazier
> **Message:** Hey, hero! Come by my office
> and pick up your fan mail. It's starting to
> pile up!

Altogether, during the weeks that followed, there would be a total of twelve greeting cards, five letters, seventeen postal cards, and one Postalette with a matching rosebud seal.

All in all, there were some pretty nice cards and letters from well-meaning citizens, a few indecipherable ones from obvious kooks, and, most surprising of all, a check for $2,000 from a retired school principal named Mrs. Laverne Livingstone, who resided near Austin,

Texas, and who subsequently had her checkbook confiscated by her horrified children. *("Well, this is it!" they exclaimed. "This will never do! We certainly can't have Mother sending $2,000 checks out willy-nilly to everybody and his brother! And just for good measure, we'd better have her examined again by Dr. Forsby.")*

The note to Blue that was attached to her check was very sweet, however, expressing thanks for his "most heroic act on behalf of grateful high school principals everywhere."

Blue was absolutely flabbergasted and didn't know what to make of it. Should he keep the check or send it back? And if he kept it, what would he use the money for?

He decided to ask Omaha out for coffee and discuss it with her. (Blue was not yet in the habit of drinking coffee, but just the idea of sitting and talking with Omaha at a corner table in the little espresso café in the Fairhaven Shopping Mall made him feel like every breath he took was made up of little molecules of happiness.)

But Blue was in for one mammoth surprise. It happened a few minutes after they had entered the completely controlled atmosphere of Fairhaven Mall—the huge expanse of gleaming imitation marble beneath their feet, the potted plants in bloom and full-grown trees with their graceful limbs reaching up to the high-vaulted glass ceiling of the magnificent structure, the soft music emanating from hidden speakers, the complete absence of anyone even slightly resembling a "street person"—all this adding up to an atmosphere of luxury and pampered safety—until they rounded the corner by The Toy Shop and came face-to-face with a six-year-old kid named Kevin McCollister.

Because he had begged for one, and to keep him quiet, Kevin's mother had just purchased a realistic-looking Uzi machine gun that shot out a simulated red lightning bolt and rat-a-tat-tatted like the real thing. But Kevin made a serious mistake: He sighted on Omaha Nebraska Brown when she was within five feet of the gun's muzzle. Rat-a-tat-tat! it went, and Omaha sprang into action like a wounded tiger.

"What do you think you're doing, you brainless little creep!" she said, grabbing the toy gun out of Kevin's hands with a jerk. "Don't you know guns *kill people*, for *#%! sake! Don't you ever, *ever* point a gun at anybody again, or I'll personally wring that *#%! filthy little neck of yours until your eyes pop out!"

Kevin's mother appeared just then, carrying a large plastic shopping bag bulging with purchases. "What's going on here, Kevin—," she started to say, nervously eyeing Omaha and tentatively reaching out to reclaim her son's Uzi.

Omaha countered by immediately slamming the toy gun on the shiny artificial marble linoleum and then jumping on it with both feet. Bits of black plastic flew up around her knees, while several large pieces of the gun skidded across the floor and came to rest against a ceramic bench built in the shape of a pretzel.

Kevin's mother took several steps backward, catching her son by the hand and glaring at Omaha. "What—what—," she started to say, but Omaha immediately took the initiative. "Are you really this kid's *mother?*" she demanded intently, not raising her voice but speaking in a firm and clear tone. "My God, lady, you're supposed to know better! Where is your poor excuse for a *#%! brain, you sorry, dumb idiot! Don't you know what guns *do* to people! Guns *kill!* A gun is not a toy! Your dumb-headed little brat *pointed* that thing at me!"

"But this *is* just a toy!" the woman said in a whining,

defensive voice. "You can't get killed by a *toy*, and you have no right—"

"Oh, yeah—*yeah!*" Omaha interrupted, curling her lip. "Just a *toy!* That's *great*, isn't it? That's just *dandy!* Just a *toy*, huh? Well, let me hear you say that ten years from now, when you find your little darling here either rotting away in a cold prison cell or lying in the street somewhere with his bullet-strewn body blown wide open and his bloody guts spilling out all over the pavement!"

Omaha exhaled in a kind of a snort and quickly looked around for Blue. She didn't have to look far. He was mesmerized, still glued to the spot where he was standing when it all started. Was he dreaming or what? Could it be that Omaha, too, was incensed by the stupidity of the American people in not acting to control the widespread illegal use of guns in this country?

"Oh, what's the use!" Omaha was saying. "Some people just don't get it! What do they care how many poor innocent slobs get shot on the street! Come on, Blue," she said, beginning to plow her way through the center of the growing crowd.

But Blue, sensing the need to forestall future unpleasantness, suddenly switched into his Avenger

72

mode. He swiftly extracted a ten-dollar bill from his wallet and handed it to the boy's mother, at the same time twirling one finger around and around at the side of his ear—the universal sign indicating a screw loose somewhere in the noggin. Then, spotting the back of Omaha's red jacket just before she was swallowed up by the crowd, he dashed after her, and in a few seconds they were hurrying hand in hand toward the café at the other end of the mall.

Kevin and his mother stood there looking like they had just emerged from the spaceship from hell. Kevin had been completely undone by Omaha's little tirade and had started to cry, and his mother was in a daze, clutching the ten-dollar bill while picturing her little darling lying in the street with his bloody guts spilling out all over the pavement.

"Now I would call that a *pretty* amazing performance," Blue said dryly a few minutes later as they breathlessly slid into a corner booth at the Café Metropolitan. And then, remembering the sow bug, he added sarcastically, "You're certainly into stomping things, aren't you, my sweet? But you know, if she reports you to security, we're dead meat," he said rhetorically, for in fact he felt quite safe.

"Oh, God, do you think she will?" Omaha looked around nervously, then she suddenly whipped off the red Windbreaker she was wearing and turned it inside out in two quick movements, first one sleeve, then the other. She put it back on again with the plaid side showing. Then she reached into one of her pockets and took out a blue knitted cap and handed it to Blue. "Here," she said, "if you wear this—cover up that spectacular hair of yours—they'll never recognize us."

Blue grinned at her and took the cap. No one had ever called his hair spectacular before.

"I read somewhere—it was some kind of folklore book, I think—anyway, the myth is that Adaman had hair like yours." Omaha reached out and patted his head. "Red, like this."

"Adaman?"

"Adaman Eve, you know. The world's first man." She laughed. "At least that's what I used to call him, when I was small."

Blue laughed, too. "Well, I can relate to that," he said, slipping the cap over his head. "I used to think the guy who owned the circus was Barnuman Bailey."

"And don't forget that famous old movie actor, Tracian Hepburn."

"How about the explorer, Lewisan Clark?"

After the waitress had taken their order for two espressos, Blue bent his head down close to Omaha's ear and asked, "So what got into you back there, anyway? You were like a different person. And your language! Yecch! Remind me sometime to tell you about how my father used to compare bad language to messy diapers and snot."

Studies by behavioral psychologists have shown that on average, people actually hear less than one-half of the words that are spoken to them. The words *messy diapers* and *snot* completely escaped Omaha's notice, or else she surely would have asked about them. One reason was that she was thinking about Travis. But she never talked about Travis, and she wasn't about to start now. "I just don't like guns," she said simply.

"Well, hey—me too," Blue said. "But still, I think maybe kids need to have an outlet for all their pent-up aggression—for all those noes they get from people bigger and stronger than themselves. And are you sure that the theory that toy guns are harmful is really accepted by everyone these days?"

"Well, it's accepted by me," she said flatly. "And I'm sorry, but I'm not just going to stand idly by and not *do* something about it. Change has to start somewhere, you know. Maybe that kid will think twice now before he points another gun—whether it's a toy or real."

"How about water guns, then? Do you want to grab water guns out of little kids' hands and stomp them to smithereens, too?"

"No," she replied, ignoring his sarcasm. "Actually, I don't have a problem with water guns. Or even rubber-band guns—like the homemade kind, with a clothespin on one end. Do you know what I mean?"

"Yeah. I know what you mean. But why would those be different from—"

"From the kind the kid had? Well, because! A water gun, see, and a rubber-band gun, too—well—they don't *kill* people, and they don't *pretend* to. Their whole purpose is to just get people wet or sting them—"

"Or put their eyes out, possibly—"

"Oh, don't be stupid, Blue. You can't get your eye put out with a rubber-band gun. But don't you see what

I mean? With those kinds of guns, there isn't any *killing* or even *pretending* to kill. What you see is what you get. Wet or stung."

"Yes, but you don't know what the kid doing the shooting is thinking. He may be shooting water or rubber bands, but in his mind he might be shooting bullets—"

Their conversation was suddenly cut short when they both noticed a security guard with a walkie-talkie sauntering by. Blue very quietly nudged Omaha with his foot. "Yeah," she whispered, ducking her head. "I see her."

But the guard passed right in front of them without even glancing their way.

"Whew!" Omaha said, pretending to wipe her brow. "I guess that means we're out of the woods. So anyway, what did you want to show me? You said before you had something to show me."

"Oh, yeah. I do have something I want to show you." Blue took out his wallet and handed over the check and the little note from Mrs. Laverne Livingstone of Austin, Texas.

"Wow! Is this for real? Two thousand dollars!"

Omaha whistled through her teeth. "What a nice old lady! So what'll you do with the money?"

"You think I should keep it, then?"

"Well, of course, Mr. Avenger! Why not? She sent it to you, didn't she? If you sent it back or didn't cash it, you'd probably hurt her feelings really bad."

Blue nodded, considering that possibility. "Wouldn't want to hurt her feelings, that's for sure."

"Hey, I know! You could use it for some Blue Avenger–type thing."

Blue drummed his fingers on his upper lip and nodded again. "Sure, I guess I could do that." He paused, then lifted one eyebrow and asked half jokingly, "But what's a Blue Avenger–type thing, anyway?"

"How should I know? You're the B.A., not me. So what did you tell me before? That stuff about work to be done, wrongs to be righted, philosophical questions to be answered, what did all that mean?"

Blue took his cue like a pro. He sat up straight in his chair and whipped off the blue knitted cap, letting loose a cascade of red hair streaming out like a flaming torch. "Blue Avenger! Secret champion of the underdog, modest seeker of truth, fearless innovator of the unknown—"

"Yeah. That's the stuff I meant." Omaha paused a minute, looking sideways off into space. Then she placed her hand gently over his and looked deep into his eyes. "Scotu! M-sot! Fiotu!" she said in a soft and mysterious voice. *"Scotu! M-sot! Fiotu!"*

Blue knit his brows. "What's that? Japanese? I don't speak Japanese."

"It's not Japanese, Blue. They're acronyms. It could be your secret motto. Scotu—*secret champion of the underdog.* M-sot—*modest seeker—*"

"Oh, sure! I get it now. M-sot. Modest seeker of truth. And the third one. What's that third one again?"

"Fiotu. Fearless innovator of the unknown. Whatever that means," she added with a roll of her eyes.

Blue carefully refolded the $2,000 check and Mrs. Livingstone's note and put them back in his wallet. "Maybe I'll explain it to you sometime," he said. "But listen, how did you do that?"

"Do what?"

"Remember all those words and figure out the initials in your head like that. That's pretty amazing."

Omaha shrugged. "How should I know? I just have a knack for remembering things. Just one of my many talents. Extremely useful, too, don't you think? Very much in demand in the real world of business and commerce." Even as she was speaking, Omaha's body was suddenly overtaken by several physiological changes. Her blood pressure skyrocketed momentarily and her heart rate increased by almost one-third. A quick rush of perspiration covered her upper body, and her mouth was flooded by a burst of saliva—all definite signs that her body knew she was about to spill the beans even before her conscious "self" acknowledged the fact.

"You know," she heard herself saying, "I even remember my father's exact words to me the very last time I saw him, which was over five years ago." (Actually, it was five years and thirty-seven days, but Omaha didn't know that. She had remembered the *words* her father had spoken, but she didn't remember the exact date on which he spoke them.)

Blue looked up quickly. He sensed by the little tremor in her voice, the flush on her face, and the slight shaking of her hands that she was about to reveal something very personal—something very close to her heart. "What were they?" he asked quietly. "What were his last words to you?"

Omaha swallowed and rubbed her lips with her hand. "He said this: 'I have to go now, baby, and I know I'll never see you again. And because your mama's so mad at me, sure as shootin' she's going to move away with you and never leave a forwarding address. I myself am going to pursue my lifelong dream at last, which is to research and write a book about a very heroic and tragic man from long ago—a man who had the guts to stand up for what he believed, and even though they tied him to a stake and burned him alive in the public square, he refused to recant. I'll always love you, and I'm sorry it has to be this way. Take care of yourself, and keep the peace.' " Omaha shrugged. "Well, that's it," she said with a toss of her head, not understanding why she was trying to pretend that those words weren't all that important to her.

But Blue knew. He knew what it meant to lose a father. And he also knew he was about to tread on the thin ice of her emotions and if he said something inappropriate, he would fall right through and never again be allowed such closeness.

"And is that what happened?" he asked softly. "Did you and your mom really move and not—"

Omaha nodded. "My mom really hates him. She

won't ever talk about him, even when I ask her specific questions. Like, I remember every year they would have a big fight about him spending a lot of money for an airline ticket to Italy. I never understood exactly why he had to go—only that he had to visit these people— George or Don Broomo, or something like that. Mom would say, 'You just did that last year!' and Dad would answer, 'That doesn't matter! I have to go *every* year. Someday, I hope, you may understand that.' "

Blue nodded, trying to make sense out of what he was being told.

"I've asked Mom about that a couple of times," Omaha continued, "but she only looks at me as if I'm talking gibberish, and then she tells me that she really doesn't want to discuss *anything* about Johnny Brown, now or in the future."

Omaha took a sip of her espresso and then wiped her lips with her finger. "My mother's actually *happy* that he's out of her life. But you know, Blue," she whispered, "I would really like to find—"

Omaha was determined not to cry. She looked away for a moment and then tried again. "I would really like to—"

"Sure, you would," Blue broke in. "So where do you think he went? Do you have any idea?"

"I don't know. I just don't know."

"Well, did you ever try to find him? I mean, well, I thought there were groups, agencies who—"

"Hey, Blue. My father's name is *Johnny Brown*, remember? And not even a middle initial." Omaha shrugged helplessly. "No. No, I never even tried, but there must be thousands of guys named Johnny Brown. They'd just laugh at me, the people at those agencies."

Finally Blue took a deep breath and put his hand on her neck. "You're a very weird and marvelous person, Omaha. And I wish more than anything in the world that I could help you. But right now, I can't even believe I'm sitting here having an espresso with you. I don't even *drink* coffee, for God's sake. So what happened? What made me wake up one morning and decide to change my name? And if you can answer that, tell me this: What caused the big bang, anyway? Did everything really begin with a gigantic explosion of a bit of matter no bigger than the head of a pin? And where are you *from?* You talk sort of funny. Are you from Arkansas or Oklahoma or somewhere like that? Do you know Mike

Fennell? He's in our English class. He thinks he's in love with Mary Ann Olson, but she won't even look at him. Isn't there some kind of miracle medicine for acne? I'll bet if his face cleared up, she'd go out with him, and then he'd see for himself what a dinghead she is, and—"

Blue had to stop to take a breath, and Omaha leaned forward. "Are you done?" she asked. "Is it my turn now?"

He nodded, and she began. "You woke up and decided to change your name because that was the only thing you *could* do. Your thoughts and your actions are all caused by chemical reactions and electrical impulses in your brain. People may *think* they're in charge, but in my opinion, they're not—and someday brain researchers will be able to prove that very fact. I don't know what caused the big bang. I don't know if everything began with a gigantic explosion. I was born in Tulsa and lived there until I was eleven years old, but *I* don't talk funny. *You* talk funny. Of course I know Mike Fennell. And the miracle acne medicine is called Accutane. It's very expensive and shouldn't be taken by pregnant women. Now it's your turn again. Why did you become Blue Avenger, and what are your goals? What do you want to accomplish?"

Blue considered her question for a moment. Then he said, "I haven't really thought about stuff like goals. But you're right. I should. I can't just go drifting along as Blue Avenger with no plan or goals. So give me a minute and let me think."

Omaha, being an unusual person, did as he asked and just sat quietly so he could think.

"Okay," he said finally. "I believe I've got a handle on this. First, I want to help those in need of help, but I must do it secretly whenever possible."

"Why secretly?"

"Simply because I'm Blue Avenger. My namesake, the original guy I draw, or used to draw—I haven't drawn him for some time now—he always does his good deeds in secret. He wants no rewards. And I must stay true to him."

Omaha nodded. "Ah. I see. I see now why you have a problem accepting that money. But really, Blue, you couldn't have saved Mrs. Manning in secret, even if you tried. So you shouldn't feel guilty about that—or the check."

"Yes. You're right. That's true. I couldn't."

"But hey, will you let me see your drawings sometime?"

"Well, I might. If you beg and beg. But maybe you should know that my brother, Josh, says they're stupid." Blue shifted around in his seat. "But my second goal—do you want to hear my second goal, since you were the one who asked?"

"Yes." She nodded. "Course I do!"

"My second goal is that I want to discover something new and wonderful."

"Your cartoon guy did that, too?"

"New and wonderful was his middle name! The Blue Avenger was always coming up with new and wonderful stuff." Blue paused. He wasn't quite sure that Omaha would be ready for this. But then he glanced over at her, noting her self-assured calmness and the relaxed way she held her cup. Just do it, he thought (not realizing he had seen that slogan on a T-shirt during their walk to the café), and plunged right in. "I want to invent a dripless meringue," he blurted out in relief and pride. "I want to break the code and conquer forever the blight of weeping meringue. I want to make the pie of pies—a lemon meringue pie that holds its shape, with a crust that stays crisp and dry until the final piece is eaten. In short, I want to make lemon meringue pie history, and I want you by my side when I do it."

Omaha was truly speechless. Finally she nodded. "Lemon meringue pie history," she repeated blankly. And then she turned her head slightly away from Blue in an obvious attempt to hide a look of utter incredulousness. "Lemon meringue pie history," she repeated to the wall. "Holy Moses."

Blue shrugged helplessly. "Laugh if you must." He sighed. "That's just what I want to do."

"Well, okay. If that's what you want, go for it."

They were both still for a moment, paying silent tribute to the perfect meringue pie.

After a pause Omaha asked, "So, is that it? Is that your entire agenda?"

"Oh, no," Blue said, expelling the air from his lips as if he were exasperated with the question. "That's just the beginning—the tip of the iceberg, as they say. Take the gun problem, for instance. I agree with you about that, even though I haven't taken the matter up in my own hands yet—no, make that *feet*," he added in a whisper, quickly glancing behind his shoulder. "But I do agree with you. It's stupid. There has to be a way to solve it. And how about medical care and dental care, too? Something's really wrong when millions of people can't afford to get hurt or sick in a country as rich as ours. Take poor Mike, for instance. Mike Fennell?" Blue paused, questioning.

Omaha nodded, slightly annoyed. "I told you, I know him from English class, remember?"

"Yeah, well, when he was two years old, his father ran off with some woman he met at a cat show, and Mike has only heard from him *once* since then. Can you believe that? It's like he just *forgot* he had kids! Anyway, Mike's poor mother is trying to support him and his two older sisters by cleaning houses and baby-sitting. They don't have any kind of health insurance at all. He told me once that except for school shots he got at a clinic, he's never been to a doctor in his life. And as for him getting treatment for those monster zits, well, you can forget *that*."

Blue took a deep breath, raised his hands above his head in a long, drawn-out stretch, and then suddenly began to smile—for something amazing was starting to happen in his brain. In a mysterious process yet to be understood in the infant field of brain research, an idea was hatching within the spongy gray matter inside his skull.

"Well, that's a cool agenda," Omaha remarked during the pause. "Is there anything else?"

"Oh, no, that's about the size of it, except for the ultimate challenge of my life," Blue answered calmly.

"Aha! So out it comes at last—your ultimate challenge. Which is?"

"Which is to solve the puzzle of puzzles, to correctly answer the sixty-four-dollar question, to crack the toughest customer in the nut bowl of life—"

"Out with it! Out with it! I can't take the suspense any longer!"

"All right, then, here it is, the question of questions: *Are we truly the masters of our fate or merely actors on a stage, playing our parts in a predetermined cosmic drama over which we have no control?* You must agree, that is the mystery of mysteries, the question for the ages, the—"

Omaha rested her elbows on the table and wearily put her chin in her hands. "My dear Blue," she said with a sigh, looking directly into his eyes. "I've already given you my opinion on that, and you don't even remember it. Of course we have choices in this life! We make them every day! But—and here's the *real* question—do we have any choice in choosing the choice we choose?"

Then she looked at her watch. "But it's getting late, and I must head for home."

Blue had a sudden urge to throw his arm around Omaha's shoulders, something that David Bruce Schumacher might have thought of but would never have had the nerve to do. For Blue, however, the maneuver was easy as pie. He was amazed at both the softness of her hair touching his bare arm and the firmness of her shoulder muscles beneath his fingers. And then Blue had another sudden urge—an uncontrollable urge to tease. He bent his head toward Omaha's ear and whispered, "Omaha Nebraska, there's something I must confess to you."

"Yes?" she answered cautiously. "And what is that, may I ask?"

"You say that our fates are sealed, and there is no use fighting destiny. The fact is, I can feel the truth in your statement even as we speak. Our chemicals are in place and our hormones are growing ever more insistent with each passing moment. You are going to end up alone in a motel with me, and sooner than you think."

Omaha couldn't have been more surprised if Blue had suddenly levitated up to the clouds, waving his handkerchief to those on the ground as he rose. The color drained from her face, and her breath caught in her throat. But after several seconds she came to recognize the wildly satirical humor behind his roguish remark, and slowly she began to return to normal. Nevertheless, the prospect left her speechless, and the only response she could muster was an exaggerated look of rampant, incredulous panic.

six

By the time Blue got home from the mall, the Accutane Project was fully hatched in his brain, but he couldn't begin to put it into effect until morning.

The next day he made the phone call during the first opportunity he got, after his second-period class. He rushed to the pay phone near the gym and looked up the number he needed.

"Medical Society," said the voice on the phone. "May I help you?"

"Yes, please. I hope so. Can you give me the name of a dermatologist in the San Pablo area, one who is taking new patients?"

He was given three names and promptly called the first one on the list, a Dr. José Alvarez.

Due to a last-minute cancellation, Blue was able to make an appointment for 4 P.M. that very afternoon.

"Your name, sir?" asked the appointments secretary.

Now Blue was in a pickle! Fearing he might be dismissed as some prank-playing teenager, he decided he must take evasive action. "My name," he said, "is David Bluvenger."

"All right, Mr. Bluvenger. We'll see you at 4 P.M. this afternoon."

Naturally, Dr. Alvarez had never heard of a proposition such as the one Blue put forth. At first he was quite skeptical, but he was soon won over by Blue's sincerity and enthusiasm. "So, let me get this straight," he said finally, leaning back in his chair. "I will offer to treat this young friend of yours for no fee—out of the kindness of my heart, I'll tell him—while in fact, you are willing to foot the entire bill, including the cost of the medication. Is that correct?"

"Yes, sir. That is correct. But it must be our secret. This must be in strictest confidence. I'll need your word on that."

Dr. Alvarez nodded. "Yes. I understand. But do you realize the kind of money we're talking about here—uh, what did you say your name was?" he asked, glancing at his clipboard. "David Something?"

The moment of truth had arrived. Blue cleared his throat. "My name is really Blue Avenger, Dr. Alvarez." He held up his hand. "Now wait, I know that sounds strange. But see, I just changed it a couple of weeks ago. I changed my name from David Schumacher to Blue Avenger. You can do that, you know. You can change your name—"

Dr. Alvarez put his clipboard down on the counter. "Hey, are you that kid who jumped into the swimming pool with the teacher? I saw your picture—"

Blue sighed with relief. It would be smooth sailing now. "Yes. That's me." He pulled out the check from his admirer in Austin, Texas, and handed it across the desk to the doctor. "A woman sent this to me—"

"Two thousand smackers! Why? Do you know her? What is she, nuts or something?"

Blue stiffened slightly and, by his expression and demeanor, conveyed his annoyance at this uncalled-for insult of his benefactor.

His reaction was not lost on the doctor. "Well. Well, then—" Dr. Alvarez said, handing back the check. "Where did you say your friend worked? And what was his name?" he asked, reaching for a pad of paper.

"You can find him every Saturday at that Taco Bell on—oh, gee, I forget the name of the street. It's just about three blocks from here, down by the library—"

Dr. Alvarez looked up suddenly and pushed away the pad of paper. "My God, I've seen that kid! Straight brown hair? Solid muscular type?"

Blue nodded. "Yep. That's him."

"*Bad* case! A real *classic* case! But luckily of a type highly responsive to Accutane." Dr. Alvarez smiled. "This will be kind of fun. The boy's name is—"

"Mike. Mike Fennell."

Dr. Alvarez stood up and pushed back his chair. "I'll stop by the Taco Bell on Saturday and offer to treat him, as you say, for free. He'd be foolish to pass up an opportunity like this. So here," he said, reaching again for the pad. "Jot down your address and I'll send you the bill."

Blue did as he was asked, then handed back the pad.

"You're positive you want to do this now?" the doctor asked, slipping the pencil behind his ear. "But wait," he said suddenly, snapping his fingers. "What about insurance? I should have asked you about that in the beginning. Do you think there's a possibility that his family—"

"No," Blue said. "They have no insurance. His mother cleans houses, and his father—well, there's no insurance."

Dr. Alvarez clucked his tongue and nodded. "That's tough. That makes it tough." He tore the top sheet off the little pad and read it aloud. "Blue Avenger, huh? Well, well, well. You'll be hearing from me in several weeks. I must say, I've never had—well, this will be a first, that's for sure."

After Blue left, Dr. Alvarez remained in his office enclosure for several minutes, because he was not quite prepared to see his next patient. He was thinking about a summer's day in a bygone year when he was sixteen and had to lock himself in the bathroom for an hour and a half so his sisters wouldn't see him crying. That was the day he had finally found the courage to ask the beautiful Gracie Bowles if she would like to go out with him. She had stared at his face for a full ten seconds before replying in a most mean and condescending tone, "No *way,* José!" Then, after laughing at her own cleverness, she added, "*Bleah!* You look *disgusting!*"

Dr. José Alvarez smiled. Someday, after the kids were in bed, he would get around to telling that story to Marie, his sweet wife. And by the time he does (and unbeknownst to him, of course), Gracie Bowles will have already moved into her penthouse apartment in La-La Land, the luxurious condominium built upon the beach in beautiful southern California, kissed by the waters of the blue Pacific.

★ ★ ★

On his way home from the doctor's office, Blue stopped by the bank to deposit the check in his savings account—an account that his grandmother had optimistically opened for him on his tenth birthday with a starting amount of $25. Mrs. Livingstone's check for $2,000 suddenly boosted his total up from $382.55 to $2,382.55.

As he walked out of the bank and started for home, Blue decided the time had come for him to get a job. While David Schumacher didn't mind accepting a small allowance from his mother, especially since he spent every Saturday looking after Josh, things were different for Blue Avenger. He had just spent more than fourteen dollars at the mall, keeping Omaha out of trouble and buying their espressos, and it would be his pleasure to spend more on her as time went on. Blue Avenger doesn't ask his mother for dating money.

He broached the subject that night after Josh had gone to bed. "I think I'm going to start looking for a job, Mom," he said. "Not on Saturdays, of course. But I still have evenings and all day on Sundays."

Her initial motherly response, of course, was negative. But she remembered the terms of their long-standing agreement and answered with an upbeat, "Oh!

Well, what kind of a job are you thinking of? Fast food—something like that?"

"Yes. I think so. Maybe Taco Bell. Maybe Mike can get me on." Blue gently bit his tongue. Oh, how he longed to tell his mother about his secret plan for Mike! He valued that special smile of approval he knew it would evoke, but he must be true to the Code: Blue Avenger always does his good deeds in secret.

The next afternoon, during his fifth-period class, Blue received an urgent memo from Mr. Frazier, hand-delivered by Omaha Nebraska Brown, counselor's office assistant:

To: Blue Avenger
From: Mr. Frazier
Message: I need your help! Please come and see me at your earliest convenience, preferably at the beginning of next period.

Omaha waited while Blue read the short message, and when he was finished, she asked if he had an answer.

"Yes. You can tell him I'll be there. But hey, Omaha,

do you know what this is about?" he asked in a low whisper, catching her arm.

"Can't discuss it," she said, doing her best to suppress a smile and at the same time rolling her eyes around wildly.

After class Blue dutifully hied himself over to his counselor's office as requested.

"Ah, Blue! Nice to see you. Sit down, m' boy. I've got a problem I'm hoping you'll be able to help me with," Mr. Frazier said, motioning to the chair opposite him and pulling a manila folder out of his desk drawer.

"Oh? Like what, Mr. Frazier?"

"Like this," Mr. Frazier replied, unfolding a large sheet of paper. "Just take a gander at this," he said, holding it up at eye level for Blue to see. "It's the proposed front page of next week's *Gladiator*, unless you can talk Rod Wilkins and the rest of those bozos on the staff out of it. As of now, though, he's got them all in his pocket."

Mr. Frazier sighed and popped a piece of chewing gum into his mouth. "Fran Manning really did a job on me this year. I mean, I don't mind taking a class or two—after those latest budget cuts there's no longer any such thing as a full-time counselor. But journalism instructor and adviser to the paper—well, that was really a low blow—"

Blue nodded sympathetically, but most of his attention was still focused on that proposed front page, and his eyes were popping out. (A fairly gruesome term—again, not meant to be taken literally.)

CONDOMS? HOW TO DO IT? NOTHING TO IT!

Beneath the headline were several larger-than-life drawings of the organ in question, before, during, and after donning the protective device mentioned above.

"Holy Moses!" Blue exclaimed, unconsciously repeating Omaha's favorite phrase for expressing surprise and not realizing he was doing it. "That's—that's really, uh, actually, that's really sort of *obscene*, in a way, isn't it, Mr. Frazier? I mean, what is that *for*, anyway?"

"It's supposed to accompany an article on AIDS—a very well-written three-part story, I might add. I have absolutely no problem with the article—it's just this, uh, this *graphic* set of drawings—I'm telling you, Blue, when Milton Blakeley sees this, bango! There goes the grant—

lock, stock, and barrel—and no *Gladiator* for the rest of the term."

"How's that?" Blue asked. "What's Milton Blakeley got to do with it?"

"Money, Blue. It's the money. The only reason we can publish a paper at all this year is because of the grant from Blakeley Brothers Supermarket."

"Oh, yeah. I guess I remember something about that, come to think of it—"

"Well, the Blakeleys have been fairly low-key about their support. It's just one of their many civic contributions—but they'll never sit still for this. They'll never allow themselves to be associated with something like this, being a family supermarket and all. But Rod Wilkins—you know him, Blue? He can be a real pain in the *#%! sometimes—"

Blue nodded. "Yeah. I know him. And I know what you mean."

"Well, he's the editor, and it's gone right to his head. He's got the publications committee all hepped up, squawking free speech and all that claptrap. I'm telling you, Blue, I'm in a bind. If I lay down the law and censor this thing, he'll have the whole school down my throat—which, I suspect, is exactly what he's after. But if I let it go, Blakeley Brothers will bail out for sure, we'll lose the paper, and I'll get the heat for not exerting proper authority. It's the old rock and a hard place situation, and I'm squeezed in the middle."

Blue nodded solemnly. He knew Rod Wilkins for what he was—a glib but intelligent attention seeker, determined to make a name for himself no matter what the cost.

"How much time do I have?" Blue asked. "I'll need to mull this over—"

"We go to press on Tuesday morning. You have until Monday afternoon, at the latest."

Blue stood up, his features suddenly chiseled in stone. "All right, sir," he said. "I'll see what I can do."

"Thank you, Blue. I'm counting on you, son."

Meanwhile, that same afternoon—in just *one* of the millions and billions and trillions of real-life "coincidences" that occurred that day but that, when they happen in books or movies, are blindly labeled "contrivances of plot" and are seemingly unfathomable by certain shallow-thinking, befuddled, and incompetent reviewers and critics—that same afternoon found Sally Schumacher—in her capacity as a certified dental hygienist—dutifully scraping six months' accumulation of bacteria-infested plaque from the teeth of Mrs. Pauline Blankenship—civil rights attorney and partner in the law firm of Greenwood, Miller, and Blankenship, as well as wife of Dr. Milton P. Blankenship, one of the country's foremost experts on malaria and other infectious diseases and an elected member of the Oakland City Council.

Being a typical lawyer, Mrs. Blankenship insisted on chatting even as Sally was endeavoring to practice *her* profession in a timely and diligent manner. But this time Sally backed off, allowing the shiny silver tool in her hand to droop while she nodded attentively at Mrs. Blankenship's every word. For Mrs. Blankenship was voicing her desperate need for a reliable and personable teenage boy to look after Lance and Vance—the rambunctious Blankenship twins—several evenings a week. Upon hearing this news, Blue's mother gently shook the silver scraper as if it were an extension of her index finger and said, "Pauline" (for this was an informal office), "your problems are over. I know the perfect guy."

seven

Just seventeen days after his father's death, Blue's grandmother also passed away—of a broken heart, they said, although the real reason was septicemia, or blood poisoning, caused by an accidental puncture wound from a contaminated embroidery needle. (Grandma Schumacher was only the eleventh person in her immediate bloodline to die of that disease, the first being a female ancestor who lived 82,592 years ago in a part of Europe that until recently was called Yugoslavia, but which was then a dangerous and inhospitable land. She was punctured in the foot by a plant of the hawthorn family, which became extinct before plants were given names. Of course, she wasn't wearing any shoes.)

The death of his grandmother left Blue's entire family numbering only four—himself, his mother, his younger brother, and his uncle Ralphy, who owned and operated a two-chair barbershop on Broadway, not far from Blue's house. Uncle Ralphy was a fair to middling barber, but his first love was engines. He spent all his spare time in his greasy blue coveralls, fooling with old cars and motorcycles, some of which he actually got to running again. He loved raising a little *#%! now and then, and he was positive that his brother, Walter, was much too straitlaced and strict with young David and Josh. "Hey, Walty baby," he would often warn, "better loosen up with those kids or you'll end up with a couple of namby-pambies for sure." Blue still remembered the exciting ride on the back of Uncle Ralphy's motorcycle when he was only five, the wind blowing through his hair and his T-shirt flapping, and the absolute fit his father threw when he heard about it. Ralphy and Walter were often on the outs, and after that ill-conceived episode, they were even further out. As for Ralphy and his sister-in-law, Sally, well, the only thing those two had in common was that they were both (in the words of the English poet) "unfeather'd two-legged things." Of course, after the cone-and-spider tragedy, Uncle Ralphy was always glad to see David and Josh drop by his shop, and their haircuts were always "on the house."

The year preceding David's metamorphosis to Blue Avenger had been a time of confusion and pessimism for him, and Uncle Ralphy's no-nonsense attitude had a leveling influence. David's main problem was that nothing seemed to make any sense anymore. It was as though the world around him and the people inhabiting it were growing more insane every day, and he was doomed to stand and watch, unable to stem the tide. Occasionally he would go to the movies with Mike or his other friends and observe in puzzled silence as the people around him screamed and hollered and jumped out of their seats every time someone on the screen was blasted to bits or slashed into mincemeat or impaled with a sharp stick. And real life was almost as bad. There was an epidemic of car thefts in his own neighborhood and even more vandalism and gang activity at his school. But most of all he was appalled to read of the increased incidence of schoolyard killings all across the country.

He tried to explain these feelings to his uncle in the language he felt he would understand. "Seems like everyone's gone nuts, Uncle Ralphy," he said one afternoon. "What are we supposed to do about that?"

"You fight it, Davey!" Ralph said vigorously. "You do what you can! Somebody says something crazy, you set him straight. That's the only way."

Three weeks later, with Uncle Ralphy's words converted into chemicals and stirred into the mix in Davey's brain, the transformation took place. David Schumacher became Blue Avenger.

The next time Blue showed up at the barbershop, Uncle Ralphy gave him the once-over. "You're looking a bit *too* shaggy, kid," he said. "Come on, sit down here before I get a paying customer."

As luck would have it, one of the regulars did come in a few minutes later and sat himself down in the empty barber chair to wait his turn.

"So how's it going, Nick?" Uncle Ralphy asked, tossing a folded newspaper onto the man's lap. "Be finished here in a minute."

Nick loosened his belt and opened the paper, happy for the chance to take the weight off his feet and get a little breather.

"*#%! red curls," Uncle Ralphy muttered. "Slippery as eels."

"How about those big crooks in Washington, not an honest one in the bunch!" Nick remarked, turning the newspaper page with a snap.

Blue cleared his throat. "Well, uh, we elected them, didn't we?" he suggested mildly. "That is, I mean, the voters elected them, right? Maybe the trouble with democracy is that it can only work well with an electorate that thinks."

Nick looked up, surprised at this unsolicited comment from the kid in the chair, since the usual response to his routine condemnation of government was a resigned look and nodding head.

"If unscrupulous politicians are elected, whose fault is it?" Blue persisted. "Maybe some other form of government would be better, since—"

Nick's face flushed. "Listen here, sonny boy!" he interrupted in a sudden and unexpected turnaround. "Our system of government is the best in the world, and don't you ever forget it!"

Uncle Ralphy removed the striped covering from around Blue's neck and brushed some loose hairs off his shoulders. Then he patted him on the back and whispered, "Attaboy!" in his ear. He was mighty proud of his nephew's style, the way he had old Nick on the ropes like that. Say, the kid was turning out to have some guts after all!

That night just before bed, Blue read two interesting articles juxtaposed on page five in the business section of the newspaper. The first one was about a mediocre rock group whose members had each made in excess of one million dollars over the previous six months, and the other documented in numbers and graphs the shrinking buying power of the nation's working poor. Not counting the assistant editor at the paper (who had slyly placed the stories side by side), only Blue and a seventy-eight-year-old retired economist in El Cerrito noticed and appreciated the irony of the situation. Everyone else was too busy watching television.

It was Saturday morning, and Blue had a job to do. In truth, he had two jobs to do: He had to baby-sit his brother, and he had to figure out a way to save the *Gladiator* from an almost certain untimely demise and Mr. Frazier from a ton of grief. Well, he asked himself, what would The Blue Avenger do in such a situation? How would his cartoon hero save the day? Blue racked his brains and tore his hair (two more vivid and imaginative phrases not meant to be taken literally) until finally he came up with a plan—a gamble so daring and unusual, it just *possibly* might succeed.

First he called up Omaha. "I've got to go to the Target," he said, "on Blue Avenger business. Would you like to come along?"

"Ah," she breathed. "The assignment from Mr. Frazier—"

"That is correct, my child. You have a sharp and excellent mind. One small problem, though. My brother, Josh, must tag along."

"Oh," she said after a short pause, a pause that Blue instantly misinterpreted.

"That's not all right with you?" he ventured, jumping to conclusions, since it really wasn't all right with *him*, but there was nothing he could do about it. His mother worked on Saturdays, and his job was looking after Josh—not letting him out of his sight for a moment, because that was the kind of kid Josh was.

"No, that's fine with me."

"Really? But you paused—"

Omaha was not yet ready to talk about Travis, but thoughts of him were what caused the pause, evoked by the simple word *brother*. "Well, I didn't mean to pause. I don't think I paused."

Blue paused, considering whether or not to pursue the subject.

"*You're* pausing now, Blue," she accused. "Hey, now *you're* pausing."

"I'm not pausing. I'm—"

"Yes?"

They both paused, neither one of them having the slightest inkling about what was going on in the other's noodle.

Oh, Love, elusive Love, what unknown hurdles you must surmount in your struggle to survive!

"Listen, Joshy, I'm going to buy some condoms, and I'm telling you now, I can do without *any* sappy comments from your direction," Blue stated, his head held high and his eyes looking straight ahead. "The fact is," he added in a defensive tone, "I need them for school."

"Oh, *right!* Yuk yuk yuk!" Josh feigned raucous laughter, holding his hands over his wide, grinning mouth. "And just what class is that, *Da*-vid?"

Omaha glanced quickly at the freckle-faced kid bobbing alongside them, first three steps ahead, then two behind. He was a cute little guy, with his blue baseball cap and Bart Simpson T-shirt, but his eyes were full of the devil.

"Just try to ignore him, Omaha," Blue said, taking her by the hand. "If you can."

The doors to the Target were automatic, and as they opened, the three of them squeezed in together. As they emerged on the other side, Josh stumbled around momentarily with his arms pinned to his sides and his breath sucked in, pretending he had been squished in the door.

"Hmm. I wonder what department those, uh, those things are in," Blue murmured, ignoring his brother's shenanigans and glancing around the store.

"Uh, how about—*menswear!*" Josh said, with an innocent, deadpan look—which he could hold for just a second before falling into an uncontrolled fit of laughter.

But even Omaha had to smile. The kid was a gas.

Up and down the aisles they went, searching for the rubbers. Past the racks of shoes and videos, automotive supplies, towels and bath accessories, greeting cards and books, adhesives, hooks, picture frames and stepladders, and rows and rows of toys—

All of a sudden, where was Josh?

"Oh, my God!" Blue exclaimed, for out of the corner of his eye he had just spotted the blue baseball cap and Bart Simpson T-shirt in the act of picking up a Kalashnikov AK-47 and starting to take a practice aim in Omaha's direction. Anticipating the mayhem that was about to engulf them all, Blue sprang into action. Joshy Schumacher didn't know what hit him, but suddenly the gun was back on the shelf and someone had him—no, not by the collar, but, more precisely, by the ribbed neck of his T-shirt, stretching it permanently out of shape.

"Hey, watch it, man! What do you think you're doing?" Josh said loudly, grabbing at his throat. "You almost choked me!"

"Yeah, yeah. I know. Just don't touch the toys. Come on."

The three of them walked on, up and down the rows. Women's hair-care notions, curlers and hairnets, then Handi Wipes, Kotex, Tampax, and, at last, at the end of that row, the condom display.

"That's weird," Omaha remarked. "What are they doing here anyway, next to all this *women's* stuff?"

Josh, meanwhile, was peering wide-eyed at the little boxes hanging in neat rows on long hooks. "Trojan, Sheik, Ramses," he read, fingering the little packages of condoms until they were all dancing gently on their hooks. "Wow! This is *neato!*"

"Get away from those, Josh," Blue said. "Don't touch the boxes."

"And look at this one! Gold Coins! They're wrapped up to look like coins!" Josh lowered his chin and began speaking in a deeper voice. "Ah, miss, let me get that parking meter for you. Whoops! Sorry! Ahem—wrong coin here—"

"Josh, I'm warning you—"

Was Josh listening? Of course not. He let out a delighted yelp and quickly slipped a small package off its hook and waved it in Blue's face. "Hey, David." He laughed loudly. "Look! These are for you! Look! *Magnum! Size extra large!* Woo-woo! Hubba-hubba!"

Blue's face turned bright red, and now he spoke between clenched teeth. "Josh, I said I'm *warning* you! So stop it! Put those right back! Right *back*, I say!" He made a grab for the little package, but Josh was too quick for him.

"Ha ha! Missed me!" Josh teased, backing away, still waving the box of Magnum condoms in the air. "These are for my brother," he told a pair of passing shoppers. "He says he needs them for school. And look," he added, tapping the little box, "size *extra large!*" He pointed at Blue. "That's him, right there. See? That big guy over there. That's my brother, all right—"

114

Blue was simply mortified. He leaned up against a support pillar in the middle of the aisle and shook his head, starting to gesture for help from Omaha. But he couldn't believe what he saw. There she was, one hand on her forehead and the other on her stomach, laughing like a fool.

Meanwhile, approximately fourteen hours away by automobile, in the Washington State Penitentiary at Walla Walla, Washington, romance was in flower. Travis had proposed marriage, and his lady friend, called Peaches Calhoun, had accepted joyfully. They had met through a "Mix 'n Match" column in *TELL-it & SELL-it*, a little weekly advertising sheet printed on yellow paper and given away at doughnut shops and coin-operated laundries. This was the ad that did the trick:

> SWM, 25, 6', 175 lbs, blond, sincere, good-looking & doing time. Searching for that "certain someone" for permanent relationship, hopefully marriage. ME, extremely fun-loving extrovert, nonsmoker but open-minded if you do, handy with hands,

can-fix-anything type, loves Astaire-Rogers movies, popcorn, and thunderstorms, ready for that "lasting relationship" with YOU, S/DWF, 21–30, understanding, patient & bold risktaker willing to take a chance on me, becuz I really need you, baby, and together we can make it happen. (Box 34)

Peaches was unaware of the fact that the advertisement was not composed by Travis himself. Rather, it was knocked out in three minutes flat by his brilliant roommate, Dalton Winger—the same Dalton Winger who was on the verge of perfecting the most revolutionary advance in personal weaponry since the club replaced the fist. For on that very day, Dalton Winger's brother, Roger, was at home in his workshop fabricating the next-to-final prototype of an elegant device that had the potential to change the world, first conceived in the mind of convicted felon Dalton Winger and destined to go down in history as the "Winger Stinger."

In due time, by going through the proper channels, Travis received permission to wed, and the date was set. Peaches Calhoun's family was aghast and vowed they would never support her in such a foolish move, but she didn't care one whit about what they thought, since she had a need to be needed, and Travis needed her. As for Travis, now that he had his bride, he lacked only one thing, and that was someone close to "stand up for him" on this day of days. He *had* to have a best man. No, of course, *not* his mother, for she had practically disowned him! No, the one person he needed and wanted was none other than his little half sister and childhood pal, Omaha Nebraska Brown.

Blue decided to wear his kaffiyeh and vest on Monday morning for his appearance before Rod Wilkins and the journalism committee. The blue towel was in the wash, but it wasn't soiled, only damp. He fished it out and secured it on his head with the piece of rope he kept in his dresser and then he slipped a twelve-pack of Trojan condoms into one of his vest pockets. That done, he went to join his mother and Josh at the breakfast table.

"Oh, puke!" Josh said upon viewing Blue in his Avenger getup. "Puke, puke, puke."

"Why, thank you, Joshy!" Blue said with a pleasant

smile, seating himself at the table. "That's very nice of you."

Josh eyed his brother suspiciously. He knew it was some kind of trick, but he couldn't stand the suspense. "Nice of me? For *what?*"

"For the compliment, of course. Didn't you just say I was cute, cute, cute?"

"Yeah! Cute! Spelled *p-u-k-e*."

"Boys, *please!* Not this morning, all right? I've got to get these checks written before I go to work, and I can't think straight with you two carrying on like that."

"Sure, Mom," Blue said, reaching for his book. "Sorry."

"Yeah, sure, Mom," Josh echoed, at the same time making a face at his brother and sticking out his tongue—an action that clearly demonstrated the difference between the unlikely hero of San Pablo High and his bratty little brother.

Blue's hold over the students at San Pablo High was still as secure as ever. The girls thought he was cute, the boys found him nonthreatening, and they were all strangely fascinated and entertained by his unique personality and approach. His sudden and unexpected appearance during second-period advanced journalism class was greeted with shouts and applause. He took his stance at the front of the room and modestly raised his palms in appreciation and thanks.

"Thank you. Thank you very much," he said. "It's an honor and a pleasure to be here among the journalistic elite. You are all, without question, *the* most intelligent and powerful people on this campus."

More applause and whistles from those fourteen students assembled in advanced journalism class that Monday morning. (Mr. Frazier, their teacher and administrative adviser to the paper, was conspicuous by his absence.)

"As you may have guessed, I'm here to discuss with you the proposed first page of this week's issue, and I have decided to just lay it on the line—no fancy tricks or stunts today. You guys are much too sophisticated for that, so I'm just going to give you the facts and let you—"

"They can't tell us what to do!" Rod interrupted loudly, sensing that a monkey wrench was about to be thrown into his well-thought-out plans. Rod Wilkins wanted to appear on television. He wanted to be seen as a hero, a fighter, a champion of freedom of the press. Rod Wilkins wanted to make a splash in the pond of publicity and generate fodder for his upcoming college application forms. "AIDS is no joke, and condoms save lives!" he continued. "We're just trying to give kids the information they need, for *#%! sake!"

"Yay! Yay, Rod! That's right! Yay! Yeah!" the others joined in.

"They're just a bunch of hypocrites!"

"*#%!-ing prudes!"

"They can't censor us!"

"What is this? A dictatorship or something?"

"Old Frazier's a coward! That's what he is!"

The kids were all standing now, crowding around Blue, turning into an ugly mob.

"Hold it just a second, please," Blue said calmly. He reached inside his vest and pulled out a copy of the page in question. He unfolded it and held it up for all to see. "This is it?" he asked. "This is the cause of all the fuss?"

One of the girls in the class actually blushed and modestly raised her hands to her face. For the unlikely hero of San Pablo High, it was a charming and heart-warming sight to behold. The others looked at one another, smiling nervously. Yes, they agreed. That was the cause of the fuss.

"You say this, uh—" Blue hesitated, holding the large sheet of paper at an angle as he studied it intently. "This, uh," he continued, "these instructions, rather, are *needed* to go along with Rachel's excellent article, which is in three parts, as I understand it—"

"That's right!" "Correct!" "If those rubbers aren't put on *properly*, well—" The speaker was temporarily overcome by a fit of silly giggling.

"Okay, okay, if you guys will quiet down, I want to show you something," Blue said, sitting on the edge of the teacher's desk. He reached into one of his vest pockets and took out the package of condoms. "Here you go," he said, holding it up. "Condoms, right? Any of you ever examined a package of these before? Hmm? Well, watch this." He quickly opened the package, emptied the contents in one hand, and displayed the inside printing for all to see. "These are instructions," he said, with just a hint of impatience in his voice. "*Instructions.* Very thorough and complete *instructions*." He paused, looking around the room, looking directly into the eyes of the fourteen students assembled there. "If you print *this*," he said, snapping his fingers on the proposed sheet, "Blakeley Brothers Supermarket will not send another red *cent* to this school. Parts two and three of Rachel's *excellent* article will never be seen. Kurt, your exceedingly entertaining sports columns will never be read again; Vicki, your 'Who's Who Around the School' will be kaput; and the rest of you, do you understand what I'm saying? It's not a question of censorship or prudes or dictatorships. It's simply a question of *where the money is coming from.* No money, no paper. And for what?" Blue stared knowingly at Rod Wilkins, a wordless accusation that did not go unnoticed by the others.

Then he again displayed the inside of the package, holding it up and moving his arm in a wide arc, like a kindergarten teacher displaying pictures in a book. "The instructions are all right here, gang. Plain as the nose on your face." His voice became louder, almost strident. "So what's it to be? Stupid, shameless sensationalism? Yellow journalism of the worst kind? *Tab*loid stuff?" He paused, letting that sink in. Then he added softly, with a sad, knowing smile, "Hey, you guys can do better than that."

The room was as silent as death.

"But, but—" Rod Wilkins started weakly, sputtering like a car that has just run out of gas.

"So print Rachel's story," Blue said, arms extended wide. "Save lives! And at the conclusion of the article, you add this bit of advice," he continued, making quote signs in the air: *"Notice to first-time users! It is important that you read and carefully follow the instructions included with the condoms."* And then Blue winked and added slyly, *"At least until you get the hang of it."*

After the laughter died down, Rachel reached for the proposed sheet of drawings, crumpled it into a ball, and tossed it into the wastebasket. "He's right, Rod," she said. "Blue Avenger's right." And the others all nodded in agreement.

Blue felt marvelous. For reason to emerge victorious in a clash with mob hysteria is indeed a rarity and truly a cause for celebration. Did I really pull that off? Blue thought proudly, stifling a grin. My God! What's next? I'm really on a roll!

eight

Blue's taste and olfactory receptors, working in concert with his saliva glands and the seven specific brain chemicals that will one day be recognized for their part in forming food likes and dislikes, told him it was time to make another pie. He threw open the kitchen cupboard doors and surveyed the family's accumulation of boxes, bottles, and jars. There was the baking powder, baking soda, white cider vinegar, tapioca, regular sugar, superfine sugar, Adolph's meat tenderizer, plain old flour, cream of tartar, arrowroot powder—he'd tried them all in varying amounts, and so far nothing had worked; his meringues continued to "weep" like there was no tomorrow.

Glancing around the kitchen, he noticed that the paper towel holder was empty. He removed the empty tube and replaced it with a new roll. Hey, he thought in a sudden burst of creative brilliance, paper towels! They're absorbent! They soak stuff up! Why not give them a try?

He quickly cut four paper towels into large circles just the size of the pie plate and set them aside. He made the pie crust first, and while that was cooling he began to prepare the new meringue recipe he had found in the food section of the newspaper. Even though it still wept, he liked its smoother, creamier consistency. When the first step was done, he placed the bowl in the refrigerator as directed and set the timer. Blue had made the lemon filling so many times he no longer needed to consult the recipe, and when it was done, he deftly poured the aromatic mixture into his baked crust and rinsed out the pot in the sink.

"Now the paper towels," he said aloud. Gently he placed all four of his circle cutouts directly on top of the lemon mixture. He immediately noticed that four sheets would not be enough, as the moisture from the filling was already beginning to penetrate the paper. He cut out four more circles and added them to the pile. Just then the timer sounded. It was time to finish preparing the meringue. When he had beaten the mixture to just the right consistency, he proceeded to pile it on top of the paper towels, spreading it all around until it touched the edges of the pie crust and finishing it off with some fancy swirls. Then he put the whole thing in the oven to brown, as usual.

Blue kept watch through the little glass window on

the oven door and removed the pie after sixteen minutes and thirty-three seconds, just as the meringue was lightly browned. It looked so good, the saliva glands in Blue's mouth turned to "on." But warm lemon meringue pie was not his bag, so he just paid silent homage to it for a moment and then into the refrigerator it went.

When it's completely chilled, he thought, I'll somehow try to extract the soggy paper towels from between the pudding and the meringue, and, perhaps (I-hope-I-hope-I-hope), my problem will be solved! If I can't stop the "weeping," maybe I can soak it up instead!

Blue went to his room and lay down on his bed. He reached for his current reading, the Lewis Thomas classic and National Book Award winner called *The Lives of a Cell*, and removed the bookmark from page 165. A few seconds later, in an essay called "On Probability and Possibility," he came upon the following sentences:

> The whole dear notion of one's own Self—marvelous old free-willed, free-enterprising, autonomous, independent, isolated island of a Self—is a myth.
>
> We do not yet have a science strong enough to displace the myth.

126

Blue was stunned. There was the answer he was looking for, right there in black and white, in the words of a world-renowned scientist and scholar! Free will, a myth! But then, the caveat: *We do not yet have a science strong enough to displace the myth.* So, no real proof. Just one man's opinion. Blue's brain was swimming again. How do you prove a thing like that? He closed his eyes and tried to sort things out, and in three minutes he was sound asleep.

Josh returned from his friend's house at eight minutes to five. His mom wouldn't be home until almost six, and he was *starved.* Well, what was that in the fridge? Could it be another lemon pie? Yes, indeed it was! What a lucky dude, to have a stupid brother who bakes pies! Grabbing a fork, he dug right in.

"Bleah! Phuuth!"

Dr. Milton P. Blankenship accepted a professorship at the University of California at Berkeley shortly after the publication of his second book, *Malaria and Other Infectious Diseases: An Overview.* His wife, Pauline, had already made a name for herself as a young and dynamic up-and-coming attorney. Upon their arrival in California, they both fell in love with a beautiful Cape Cod home in a very ritzy old established neighborhood high up in the Oakland hills and subsequently became the first black family to move into the area. With the twins still in diapers, Mrs. Blankenship decided to cut down considerably on her workload, at least temporarily; nevertheless, she would often find it convenient to call the Scandy-Nannies Agency for help with the babies. Most of the nannies were young Scandinavian women with temporary work permits. For the longtime residents of the neighborhood—those old conservative geezers and their aging society matron wives shuffling along the sidewalk on their daily constitutionals—it took a bit of getting used to, that tall white nanny walking to the park with those two black toddlers gurgling away in their double stroller. But in the long run, the sight proved to be beneficial for the local septuagenarians. It stimulated their tired heartbeats and got their sluggish juices flowing again. And it also exercised certain rarely used muscles and ligaments in their necks as they turned and stretched to stare at the passing spectacle.

After they had settled into the area and their circle of friends widened, Dr. Blankenship realized that he would like to become more active in the local political arena.

His friends recognized his potential, mounted a successful campaign, and Dr. Blankenship began serving his first term on the city council just four years after his arrival in town. From the beginning, he was acknowledged to be one of the most concerned, conscientious, and effective members of that body in many a moon.

Blue was honored to be hired as the Blankenships' part-time evening kid-sitter, and he turned out to be perfect for the job. However, he discovered after his first night that his biggest problem would be transportation. His hours were 7 P.M. to 10 P.M., three nights a week, and taking the bus was not only inconvenient and time-consuming but also—through certain parts of the route—downright life-threatening.

The solution was obvious; it was time for Blue to learn to drive. The problem was that with the latest budget cuts, driver education was no longer offered at San Pablo High, a fact he just happened to mention in passing while shooting the breeze with Uncle Ralphy during a drop-in visit to the shop.

"No more driver ed, huh? Well, that sure is stupid. Say, listen, Davey, why don't you come on by the house this Sunday afternoon and—"

"Blue, Uncle Ralphy."

"Blue what?"

"My name, remember? I'm Blue now."

Uncle Ralphy stared at Blue with an expression that was a strange mixture of a scowl and a grin. "Eh, you kids nowadays!" he said finally, cuffing him playfully on the ear. "Okay, *Blue*—sheesh!" he broke off, shaking his head.

"So what about Sunday?" Blue prompted. "Come by your house? What for?"

"I'll teach you how to drive, boy! Since your old man's not around anymore, I guess it's up to me. In the meantime, you can stop by Motor Vehicles and pick up your learner's permit and one of those booklets they have, with all the rules and stuff. And hey, you'd probably better check with your mom," he added as an afterthought. "Make sure it's okay with her. Matter of fact, she's probably got to sign for you. I don't know the details on that."

Blue nodded. "Right," he said. "Don't worry. I'll take care of it."

When Sally Schumacher heard the plan, not only did she approve of it but she was also relieved to find that she would be spared this chore. And as for Blue, he was simply ecstatic, which was not surprising, since the prospect of actually driving a car and getting a license has a definite stimulating effect in the brains of most American teenagers, both male and female. (In the male brain, as future studies will prove, the pleasurable anticipatory effect is closely connected with sexual desires, while in the female, the association is related more to the desire for independence. An exciting bonus for the researchers working on these future definitive brain studies will be the totally unexpected finding that those persons who insist most strongly upon the necessity of an old-fashioned traditional "plot" in books and motion pictures also have the weakest grasp on reality and are the most limited with regard to creativity and native intelligence.)

Blue hadn't been over to his uncle's place for some time and was surprised at what he found there, which was exactly seven automobiles in various states of disrepair and a backyard that looked like a wrecking yard.

"Come here, Davey," Uncle Ralphy said, wiping his greasy hands on his blue coveralls and leading the way to the oversized double garage he used as his workshop. "I want to show you something."

Blue sighed. No use fighting it, he thought. Just let him call me Davey. No use making a big deal out of it. "Okay," he said. "Wow! Where'd you get all these cars? What's that red one? Hey, isn't that an old Corvette?"

"Oh, yeah," Uncle Ralphy answered, glancing at the Corvette with a quick turn of his head. "Yeah, that's a Vette, but check this out!" He ushered Blue into the garage and stepped back a few feet so he could get an unobstructed look.

"What—what is *that?*" Blue stammered. "An old lunch wagon or something?"

Uncle Ralphy laughed. "Yeah. That's exactly what it is. Look here." He led the way around to the side of the old converted van and pointed to the slightly faded orange and blue letters painted on the dented white panel.

Wayne's Samwich Wagon
Also Serving
Coffee ☆ Soft Drinks ☆ Ice Cream
25¢ each

"Ain't that something, though! I just picked it up a couple of days ago. The guy practically paid me for getting it off his hands. Now watch this." Uncle Ralphy yanked on a little handle and swung open the large side panel, propping it up with the two metal bars that were attached to either end. "See in there? All it needs is a little work, and it'll be all set up to go." Uncle Ralphy shrugged. "Of course, that old icebox probably needs to be replaced, and that coffee percolator has seen better days. But check out all those shelves and stuff. Perfect for candy bars and potato chips. Yes, sirree! Somebody had a nice little business going for himself here." Uncle Ralphy closed the panel again, slamming it several times before the catch held. "You know what I'm gonna do, Davey boy? I'm gonna put me a rebuilt V-8 engine in that thing." He pointed somewhere toward the back of the garage. "See it over there?" He laughed. "It'll pass anything on the road when I'm finished with it. *Samwich* Wagon! Can't wait to see the surprised looks on the faces of the other drivers when I whiz by them on the freeway!"

Blue nodded gamely, trying to work up some enthusiasm, but he just couldn't seem to share Uncle Ralphy's delight in that old beat-up wreck.

"Okay, then, let's get going," Uncle Ralphy said. "I'm going to let you start out in the Chevy there, because of the stick shift. Half the kids your age haven't the foggiest notion on how to handle a *real* car. All they know is gas and brakes."

Blue felt his pulse quicken, and his breath caught in his throat. This was going to be *great!*

An hour and a half later they had finished circling around and around the large empty parking lot adjacent to an old deserted market and were now driving down a real street, heading for home, and Blue was still at the wheel.

"*Nice* going, kiddo! You're a natural!" Uncle Ralphy exclaimed as Blue maneuvered the old Chevy up the narrow driveway and into its parking place alongside the fence. "You did a really *fine* job, considering that stick shift and all. A couple more sessions and you'll be ready for your license."

"You really think so? Jeez, that's great!"

Uncle Ralphy cocked his head. "So okay. Now I gotta ask you. What's with this Blue business? Is that some kind of joke or what?"

"No. It's no joke. It's just something I wanted to

try—and, you know, it seems to be working," Blue added, in a remarkable understatement.

Uncle Ralphy pursed his lips and nodded for a moment. He was remembering back to the time when he was sixteen, which seemed like only yesterday. And he was remembering how he would have given anything back then if he could have changed his name to Rocky or Buck. Finally he shrugged and slapped his nephew on the back. "Okay, Blue," he said. "Next Sunday, then? We'll take another spin."

"Thanks, Uncle Ralphy. I'll be here. Thanks a lot. Really. I appreciate it. I *really* appre—"

Uncle Ralphy smiled, removing his cap and rubbing his chin. "Can all that *#%!, kid, and just get your butt over here next week."

On Saturday morning at nine minutes after eleven Blue got a telephone call from Omaha Nebraska Brown. "Have you seen the morning paper yet?" she asked.

"Yeah. Part of it. Why?"

"You saw 'Auntie Annie,' then?"

"No. I don't think so. What was it about?"

"You'd remember if you saw it. So anyway, go check

it out. Gotta hang up. I'm late for swimming."

Blue found the morning paper in a heap on Josh's bedroom floor and began the search for "Ask Auntie Annie," America's most popular newspaper column— and the first topic of conversation in almost every home and place of business throughout the land. (In fact, for his groundbreaking doctoral thesis in social psychology, a certain Bryan Beaverton of Clinton, New Jersey, interviewed a cross section of Americans about their activities on the morning following the devastating earthquake in northeastern Afghanistan, which buried thousands of homes perched on hillsides and killed an estimated 3,300 human beings. The most surprising finding of Bryan Beaverton's study was that the tragedy in Afghanistan was *not* among the top ten topics of discussion for a whopping 89.7 percent of the subjects interviewed. What was talked about, however, was Auntie Annie's spirited essay regarding the proper way to insert your toilet paper roll. Does the loose end extend from over the roll or under it? That was the question!)

Blue finally located the Living section and the column for which he was searching:

ASK AUNTIE ANNIE, by Annie Marzipan

Dear Readers: A question I am often asked is, to whom do *I* turn when *I* need help? The answer to that is simple: I turn to *you*, my wonderful and faithful readers! And that is exactly what I'm doing now. Let me explain: For more years than I care to admit, I have had the privilege of knowing a fine and marvelous captain of industry, Mr. Chase R. Wanner, president of the board of the Wanner Cornstarch Company. As fellow aficionados of that all-time American favorite, lemon meringue pie, Mr. Wanner and I have recently discovered that we share an identical "pet peeve"—which is, in a word, the infernal "weeping" and "dripping" that occurs whenever egg whites are whipped with sugar, piled upon a lemon filling, and baked. In other words, "weeping" meringue! So please, *someone* out there in Reader Land must have the solution to this perplexing problem. You have never failed me yet! So send me that recipe! In return you will receive a special gift from Mr. Wanner as well as ample recognition for your achievement and the accolades of a grateful nation. I'll be waiting for your recipes! Until then, please remember, to maintain a happy marriage, bathe daily (or every other day, at the very least), and always hang your toilet paper the preferred way, with the loose end extending over the roll.

Blue put the newspaper down and rapped his forehead repeatedly with his knuckles. He was still feeling dejected after the abysmal paper towel fiasco, in spite of the fact that an unsuspecting Josh turned out to be the guinea pig. But if a solution existed—and he knew it must—he simply *had* to be the one to find it!

Oh, what a burst of activity that resolution started inside his brain! The action could be described either in scientific terms or in symbolic language—the scientific terms encompassing such things as electrical waves, chemical changes, and tepkoles (a word that has yet to be coined, but truly an amazing breakthrough in the field of brain research). In symbolic terms, however, it's the little man who never sleeps and the red button at his fingertip. Ever watchful, ever alert, considering every option and every possibility, the little man will press the red button when the proper moment arrives, and Blue will respond to the alarm.

nine

"So hey, what's up?" Mike asked as he turned to wait for Blue, who was walking to school the regular way this morning, in spite of the possibility of solicitations for pocket change and smokes by the denizens of the park.

"Not a whole lot. How 'bout you?" Blue answered, struggling to keep his voice steady, for almost five weeks had passed since his deal with Dr. Alvarez and so far Mike had not said a word about the dermatologist. Habitually sensitive to the feelings of others, Blue had long avoided roving glances at Mike's face while still retaining direct eye contact whenever appropriate. But now he discreetly stole a look, and his heart skipped a beat at the sight, for the raging conflagration was being quelled at last!

Mike hesitated, then shrugged but didn't answer, at least not at first.

Blue kept quiet also, just walking along, kicking the rocks, hoping Mike would say more.

"You know, a funny thing happened—" Mike began slowly.

"Yeah? What?" Blue asked eagerly.

Mike glanced quickly at his friend and then immediately looked away. A wave of embarrassment and shyness suddenly overtook him. He had no better friend than Blue, but still he just couldn't bring himself to reveal either the fact that he had been so miserable and despondent in recent weeks that he almost killed himself or that a dermatologist appeared from out of the blue and offered to treat his awful disfigurement. Mike Fennell was born a private person and would always be that way.

"So, what?" Blue asked, gently prodding. "What funny thing happened?"

Mike sucked in his breath, slowly, slowly, stalling for time.

"Well, I dreamed about Omaha Nebraska Brown last night," he heard himself say, amazed at his own ingenuity. "Actually, I dreamed about her—"

Blue stopped dead in his tracks, positioning his feet and raising his fists. "Take that back, you asterisk, pound sign, percent, and exclamation point toady! Take that back, I say!"

Mike laughed, and they continued on toward school.

Meanwhile, alone in his office two and three-tenths miles away, Dr. José Alvarez was dictating a note to Blue, which his secretary would transcribe and send out later in the day. (The doctor would have preferred to relay the message by phone, but he didn't have Blue's number and he wasn't listed in the book.)

Dear Blue:

I have been thinking about your unusual offer to pay for the medical treatment of your friend Mike Fennell. However, after some thought, I have decided to absorb these costs myself. To witness the changes that have occurred in this patient has been payment enough. Also, you may be interested to know that I plan to make a regular practice of offering free treatment to other similarly affected teenagers who cannot afford the costs involved. Good luck in your future endeavors.

Sincerely,
José Alvarez, M.D.

As things would turn out, this lovely tradition would continue on throughout the years, even as Dr. Alvarez's son—and then his granddaughter—took over his practice, and would cease only after a comprehensive and affordable health-care plan for *all* Americans was *finally* pushed through the Congress of the United States sixty-three years later.

It was Saturday again, Lance and Vance Blankenships' eighth birthday, and Blue was enlisted to help with the party, with the proviso that Josh be allowed to tag along. Their father, the malaria expert and city council member, had to skip several important meetings in order to be with his sons on their special day. The agenda, planned by Mrs. Blankenship, called for the twenty-five party guests to be dropped off by their parents at eight thirty in the morning at the spacious parking lot adjacent to the new seven-story building housing the Benevolent Trust Altruistic Five-Way Insurance Company, Inc. There they would be met by a specially chartered FunTime PartiBus (complete with several aides in clown costumes and a plethora of balloons), which would take them down the freeway to Marine World Africa USA for a full day of fun, fun, fun.

Dr. Blankenship—feeling guilty as usual, since his busy schedule forced him to spend so much time away from his family—had agreed not only to personally deliver Lance and Vance to the parking lot but also to accompany them and the twenty-five boys on the journey in the FunTime PartiBus. (Mrs. Blankenship might or might not meet them at Marine World for lunch, according to the demands of her own busy schedule.)

Blue and Josh were the first to arrive, being dropped off early by their mother on her way to work. Josh turned out to be a problem from the start, at first even refusing to get out of the car. The reason he gave was that Blue looked stupid in his "outfit"—meaning his towel and vest—and he (Josh) didn't wish to be seen in his company. But of course he *had* to get out of the car, because it was either spend the day with Blue or hang around the dentist's office for eight hours, and that, his mother assured him, was impossible.

Because of a long-term labor dispute, the parking lot hadn't been cleaned or swept in 116 days. Blue was glad that Mrs. Blankenship was not there to see it, because she was an extraordinarily neat lady by nature, and the sight of that unkempt meeting place for her sons' party would surely be distasteful to her. At exactly eight twenty-five, Dr. Blankenship arrived with the birthday twins, and Blue quickly walked over to greet them. Since Dr. Blankenship had never once been at home during Blue's hours of duty, they had not yet had an opportunity to meet.

"Good morning!" boomed Dr. Blankenship, climbing out of the driver's seat and extending his hand. "You must be Blue. Pauline has really been bragging on *you*, I can tell ya!"

Lance and Vance fell over each other tumbling out of the backseat and ran over to Blue, each grabbing on to one of his arms and proceeding to pull him in opposite directions.

"Hey, let loose a sec." Blue laughed, shaking Lance (or was it Vance?) off his right arm and then extending it to Dr. Blankenship. "Thank you, doctor. It's a pleasure to meet you."

Several cars suddenly began converging on the otherwise deserted parking lot. Blue thought he saw a slight nervous twitch and a tightening in the older man's face as the area around them suddenly began to fill with boys—running, jumping, chasing, grabbing, screaming, pushing boys. (The boys' parents, of course, didn't waste any time getting out of there. It was just dump the kid and *varoom!*)

Soon the appointed time arrived. It was eight thirty in the morning, but, as yet, no PartiBus with clowns and balloons was anywhere to be seen.

Eight thirty-five; eight forty; now eight forty-five. The parking lot was utter pandemonium.

Oh, where, oh, where could that little bus be? At eight forty-six, Dr. Milton P. Blankenship climbed back into his car and made an urgent phone call to the FunTime PartiBus office.

"Oh, I'm so sorry, sir, but due to a—well, a sort of mix-up, like, there's going to be a slight delay. See, first the computer was down, and then we had this new girl in the office, and she originally scheduled your sons' party for *Sunday*, but then when Margo—she's the regular girl—when Margo checked the—"

"Miss!" Dr. Blankenship broke in. "What *time* will the bus arrive? There are boys running loose all over this parking lot! Somebody's going to get killed unless you get that *#%! FunTime PartiBus on out here, and I mean *pronto!*"

"Well, yes, sir, I understand, but see, we had to call our standby driver, and the clowns—well—see, they're just these college kids and we've been trying to round them—"

"*What time?*"

"Uh, well, ten o'clock? Maybe?" the frightened little voice ventured.

"That's over an hour!" The doctor and Oakland City Council member looked out the window of his car. Five of the boys were already attempting to scale the seven-foot chain-link fence, and it looked like a scuffle between several others was beginning to heat up. He hung up the phone and put his head on the steering wheel for a moment, desperately wishing he were back in the deadly snake- and malaria-infested tropics trapping infected mosquitoes—risking his future health, or, indeed, his life—instead of the position in which he presently found himself.

Finally he got out of the car and walked over to Blue, who was sitting on the asphalt writing furiously on little pieces of notebook paper that he had withdrawn from one of his numerous vest pockets.

"She told me it'll be over an *hour* before they get

here!" Dr. Blankenship said, his voice edged with hysteria. "*Now* what do we do?" asked a man who, only the night before in his capacity as an elected public official, had been partly responsible for spending hundreds of thousands of dollars belonging to the taxpayers of the city of Oakland and yet was here rendered almost useless by a group of prepubescent boys.

Blue wasn't surprised at the foul-up at the FunTime PartiBus office, since he had a gut feeling that any company that spelled its name with capital letters smack in the middle of a word really couldn't be trusted. And the FunTime PartiBus Company was doubly guilty. "You can calm down now, sir. Doctor, sir. I think I've got a plan," he replied. "I think I'll be able to handle this just fine. But I'll need—ah, let's see, ten times seven—how does seventy dollars sound? Can you spare that much to get us out of this?"

The doctor's wallet practically burst open, and the seventy dollars was produced just like *that*. "Do you need more? Here, here, take more!"

"Oh, no. Seventy is sufficient." Blue carefully folded the bills and put them into one of his vest pockets. Then he reached into another pocket and pulled out a referee's whistle. (This was one reason he loved that old fishing vest—it was so *pockety*.)

Was it something about the way he *blew* the whistle or something in his demeanor that simply charmed the little monsters and had them gathered around him in no time, like flies around a honeypot?

"Here's the deal!" Blue said, smiling broadly. "Lucky for you guys, the FunTime PartiBus is gonna be *late!*"

"Yay!" they screamed, jumping up and down. "Hurrah!"

"Because now," Blue continued, "you can play the world's newest and most exciting game—" He paused for effect. *"Parking lot scavengers!"*

"Yay! Yippee! All *right!*"

Blue quickly counted off the twenty-eight boys into four groups of seven. (Twenty-five guests, plus the twins and Josh—for even he had fallen under the spell and was being very cooperative, which was handy for Blue, because now the groups would come out even.)

Then Blue passed out the four slips of paper that he had just prepared, one to each team. "Now listen up, kids! The winning team will be the one with the most points. You'll notice that each item is worth a certain amount of points, and there is no limit to the number of items you can collect." Blue looked at his watch. "The game goes on until the PartiBus arrives, which should be in about an hour. So when you hear my whistle, I'm sorry, but it's over! And get this! The prize for the winning team is seventy bucks! For you guys who can't divide, that's ten dollars each, kids! Not bad, eh? Okay, then. The rules are simple: Stay in the parking lot, and no fair stealing stuff from other teams. Any questions?"

"Can we reach through the chain links for stuff?" asked one astute lad, spying an empty orange Jell-O box (six points) lodged in the weeds on the outside of the fence.

"Sure. As long as you stay in the lot. Any more questions? No? All set, then! Happy hunting! One, two, three, go!"

The boys quickly huddled together in their four little groups, each with a copy of Blue's list. "Let me see! Let me see!" they said, pushing and shoving and grabbing the list out of one another's hands. This is what it said:

1. Empty cigarette pack (1 point)
2. Paper clip (2 points)
3. Kit Kat candy bar wrapper (3 points)
4. Piece of blue or green glass (4 points)
5. Chicken bone (5 points)
6. Empty box or carton, no larger than a pint of milk (6 points)
7. Nut, bolt, or screw (7 points)
8. Losing lottery ticket (8 points)
9. Jigsaw puzzle piece (9 points)
10. Paper sack full of $100 bills (10 points)

Group by group they dispersed, the boys fanning out over the parking lot in an excited frenzy like starving hawks on a chicken farm.

"What *kind* of candy wrapper does it say?" they screamed to one another.

"Kit Kat! Kit Kat!"

"Here's a safety pin! Is that on the list?"

"Who's got the list? Who's got the list?"

Dr. Blankenship was utterly amazed. "Let's sit this out in the car, shall we?" he asked Blue with a smile. "We'll be more comfortable there. And listen here," he added, putting his hand on Blue's arm, "if there's *any-thing* I can ever do for you, just say the word. You are one *exceptional* kid!"

Chalk up another victory for Blue Avenger.

Two hours and five minutes later, as the PartiBus was finally heading toward Marine World with the clowns now in charge, Blue and the doctor began the not-too-pleasant task of sorting through the parking lot debris to tote up the points and determine the winning team. As Blue would call off the name of each item and deposit it into a garbage bag, the doctor would neatly keep a tab of the score.

"A nut and a bolt, fourteen points," Blue intoned. "Two paper clips and four cigarette packs, eight points. One chicken bone. Yuck. Five points. Let's see here—three pieces of blue glass and a screw. That's nineteen big ones. An empty Jell-O box—" Blue's breath caught in his throat and his heart began thumping like a jack-hammer, for the clever little man who never sleeps had pushed the red button at last. "Jell-O! Made from gela-tin!" Blue breathed. "Gelatin! That's it! That's the solu-tion! That *has* to be it!"

Blue was Mr. Popularity with the boys for the rest of the day at Marine World, and even though he enjoyed himself immensely, he found himself periodically checking his watch until it was time for the party to end.

As soon as he got home, he rode his bike to the store and bought a box of Knox unflavored gelatin, and right after dinner he began experimenting with various amounts and methods of incorporating the gelatin into the egg whites. And finally in the wee hours of the night, on his seventh try, there it was, *The Last Meringue*—Blue Avenger's Weepless Wonder Lemon Meringue Pie! Oh, joy!

The next morning found his precious recipe winging its way to "Ask Auntie Annie," and soon it would be sweeping o'er the land, bringing lemon meringue bliss to young and old of every race and creed.

ten

Blue read John O'Hara's novel *Appointment in Samarra* in just four nights. He enjoyed the book tremendously, and the Samarra legend as retold by W. Somerset Maugham under the title "Death Speaks" sent a teeny-weeny wave of electricity from certain sections of Blue's brain down through his spinal cord, a phenomenon usually described by individuals as "chills running down my spine." The quotation was printed at the very beginning of the book just as a way of explaining the title, since the novel itself had nothing at all to do with the legend.

DEATH SPEAKS

There was a merchant in Bagdad who sent his servant to market to buy provisions and in a little while the servant came back, white and trembling, and said, Master, just now when I was in the market-place I was jostled by a woman in the crowd and when I turned I saw it was Death that jostled me. She looked at me and made a threatening gesture; now, lend me your horse, and I will ride away from this city and avoid my fate. I will go to Samarra and there Death will not find me. The merchant lent him his horse, and the servant mounted it, and he dug his spurs in its flanks and as fast as the horse could gallop he went. Then the merchant went down to the market-place and he saw me standing in the crowd and he came to me and said, Why did you make a threatening gesture to my servant when you saw him this morning? That was not a threatening gesture, I said, it was only a start of surprise. I was astonished to see him in Bagdad, for I had an appointment with him tonight in Samarra.

Blue pondered the meaning of the legend. It was obvious that the servant had no choice in the matter. By rushing off to Samarra he thought he was exercising his free will, but he was actually merely fulfilling his destiny, his rendezvous with Death. Blue wondered what his father thought when he read that, and how he had reconciled it with his own opposing beliefs.

It was late, and his mother and Josh were already asleep the night he reached the final page. On the way to returning the book to his father's bookcase in the front room, Blue stopped by the kitchen and fixed himself a bowl of ice cream—being careful not to rattle the dish and closing the freezer door as quietly as he could. The O'Hara novel was a small volume—like so many of his father's books, a Modern Library edition—and before placing it back on the shelf, Blue set down his bowl of ice cream and held the book closely between his hands. *He touched this book. He touched every page*, Blue thought. It was so quiet in the house. His father's brown recliner chair belonged to all the family now. And his silver metal ashtray was on the coffee table just as before, even though there were no longer any smokers in the house. Still holding fast the book, Blue remembered the pathetic little fantasy he used to conjure up during those first few terrible weeks. Because he felt so melancholy, he tried it once again: *He's not dead. Oh, Dad, you're not dead! It's just a trick, a game, a nightmare. When I open my eyes, I'll see your cigarette, still smoldering in the silver ashtray, and watch you pound your fist into your palm as your Raiders make another first down—*

Blue Avenger blinked back the burning in his eyes and replaced the book on the shelf. He never could understand his father's love of football and always hated it when the games were on—the senseless screaming of the fans, his father's euphoria when they won ("All right! All *right!*" he'd say, as if he himself were on the team).

Sighing, Blue removed the next book in line, which was called *A Complete Travel Guide to Rome*, and, quickly thumbing through it, he noted the many photographs and hand-drawn neighborhood maps. Had he looked carefully at the inside cover, he would have seen that the book did not belong to his father at all. It had inadvertently been left behind by the former occupants of the house.

Blue picked up his bowl of ice cream, which was partly melted by then, and started for his room. He didn't even notice the small brown spider slowly making his way up the wall and into the crack beneath the wooden molding.

But then, he didn't notice the one in the bathroom, either, or the one hiding under the wastebasket in his room. Spiders are all over the place.

There was even one in a top desk drawer in a tiny garret room in Washington, D.C., crawling over an airplane ticket for Italy, for it was almost time for Johnny Brown's yearly pilgrimage to the Campo dei Fiori in

Rome—where every year on the anniversary of his death, the faithful gather at the foot of the brooding statue of Giordano Bruno to pay homage to their hero, martyred in the cause of intellectual freedom.

Five years older but steadfastly pursuing his dream, Johnny has spent his days in a quiet reading room in the Library of Congress researching materials for his book. He accomplished his first task in less than a year, and that was learning to read the Italian language, for then he was able to study the original, untranslated works of his subject—that valiant man of courage, the Italian philosopher, writer, poet, and mathematician—the pride of the Campo dei Fiori.

Living on peanut butter sandwiches and beans and working evenings in a parking garage to pay his rent, Johnny Brown had found himself at last. But always buried deep in his heart is a raw and bleeding place, and its name is Omaha Nebraska Brown.

The newspapers called it Bloody Thursday—not original, but descriptive. For on that day, nineteen human beings and one gray-striped alley cat were killed by handguns in separate incidents within the city of Oakland,

California. The public was incensed, but it was the heartless, wanton death of the cat that really got their dander up. Dat-Cat was not just any cat. He was the friendly feline that graced the premises of the Back-Alley Bar and Grill, a longtime hangout of the ace reporters of the Oakland *Star* and a favorite watering place of the city's most visible movers and shakers.

BLOODY THURSDAY MASSACRES
SENSELESS SHOOTINGS LEAVE 19 DEAD

AMONG THE VICTIMS, DAT-CAT
By Margaret Jennings, Staff Reporter

Nineteen people and one of the best-loved cats in town were left dead yesterday in the wake of the most violent outbreak of senseless shootings in the city's history.

Police Chief Charlie Owens says he has never seen anything like it. "Our guys were running around the city like chickens with their heads cut off," Owens said with a mirthless smile.

The first shooting of the day was reported at 5:37 A.M. at Dainty Donuts in the midtown area when

27-year-old Albert Phillips was killed in an altercation over the last remaining chocolate buttermilk bar in the case.

That incident was followed within the hour by a killing on Broadway when motorist Vic Lytle "cut in" in front of an unidentified man driving a red Bronco XLT. "The guy just pulled out this handgun and fired away," said Mary Hastings, a passenger in the Lytle vehicle. "Luckily I was able to grab the wheel and pull to the side of the road."

The shooting of little seven-year-old Alicia Valdez was reported shortly after 8 A.M., when a barrage of shots ripped through the front window of her parents' modest home near Lake Merritt.

"I guess she was just in the wrong place at the wrong time," a distressed neighbor said. "It's a dirty rotten shame. She always had a smile on her face and never did anything bad to anybody."

But by far the saddest faces in all the city were those seen at the Back-Alley Bar and Grill, located just around the corner from the offices of the *Star*.

"I just can't believe she's gone," wept bartender Jake Honeywell. "This big bruiser just walked into the place and shot her point-blank. After I realized what had happened, I tackled the guy and yelled for help. They've got him behind bars now, and I hope they fry the creep. I just don't know what's come over this town. Dat-Cat was the best friend I ever had."

Some confusion surfaced regarding Dat-Cat's sex when Honeywell was interrupted by an unidentified red-eyed mourner. "Hey, Honey, I thought Dat-Cat was a male."

"Well, she was," Honeywell replied, later admitting that he called every cat "she."

And even as Honeywell was talking to reporters, people from all walks of life were wandering into the Back-Alley Bar, many bearing small gifts and bouquets, to console and comfort one another.

The next tragedy occurred just before noon at Vineland School, where an eleven-year-old boy suddenly pulled out a gun in class and shot a classmate in the back. It was the third such shooting at the trouble-plagued elementary school since last September, when another eleven-year-old was shot for calling (See CAT, p. 12A)

A full-page editorial in the *Star* called for prompt action on the part of the Oakland City Council to stem this outrage and proposed a general town meeting next Monday night, presided over by the members of the city council, where individual citizens would have an opportunity to voice both their frustrations and suggestions. "If more police protection is what is needed in this city, then for heaven's sake let's quit this shilly-shallying and get on with it!" was the rousing concluding sentence.

Meanwhile, approximately fourteen hours away by automobile, in Walla Walla, Washington, the Winger Brothers were jumping with joy. The final prototype was an unqualified success, and the "Winger Stinger" was a reality at last. All it needed now was a chance.

The last five minutes of class had arrived. Ms. Chandler checked her list and called out pleasantly, "Mike? What word or quotation have you brought for our consideration today?"

Mike Fennell was momentarily stunned. He had completely forgotten about that. "Oh, *#%!," he muttered, dropping his chin down to his chest.

Ms. Chandler pursed her lips and surveyed the class

with a sweeping glance. "Well, all right," she said, turning to the board. "Why not?" And thereupon—in an act that so typified why she was such a favorite among the students—she unhesitantly wrote upon the board in large capital letters Mike's "bringaword" for the day: **S H I T**.

There was a sudden burst of laughter and looks of shocked surprise. The class was in her pocket. Oh, how Ms. Chandler loved to teach!

"And what part of speech do we have here, Mike?" she asked.

Mike began to slowly rise up in his seat. "Uh, well, it's a noun, I guess," he said quite shyly. "And also a verb. To, uh—*to shit*," he added with a blush, to the utter delight of his classmates—especially one Mary Ann Olson, who noticed with amazement that Mike Fennell's face was looking *much* better, and he was really quite a handsome stud!

Jennifer Chambers, the most serious student in the class, tentatively raised her hand.

"Yes, Jennifer?"

"There's also the adjective form—*shitty*." Then suddenly realizing she had just uttered in front of the whole

162

class a word she would never dream of using, Jennifer covered her mouth with her hand and blushed a deep crimson red.

"Yes, that's correct, Jennifer. But let's concentrate on the noun, shall we? May we have some synonyms, please?" she asked, chalk in hand. "Anyone?"

"Crap!" (Titter.)

"Turd!"

"Number two!" (Laugh.)

"Poop!" (Another laugh.)

"Dung!"

"Dingleberries!" (Big laugh.)

"Feces!" (No laugh.)

"Excrement!" (No laugh.)

"Not so fast, please," said Ms. Chandler, quickly writing *feces* and *excrement* on the board. "Okay, now I'm caught up. Continue."

"Business!"

"Droppings!"

"Scat!"

"Cow chips!"

"Cow pats!"

"Stool!"

"Ca-ca!" (One embarrassed laugh.)

"Doo-doo!" (Laugh.)

"Manure!"

"Load!"

"Guano!"

"*Guano?* What's that?"

"Oh, what an ignoramus!"

"Dung!"

"We said that one already!"

"Oh."

"Has anyone checked the thesaurus?" Ms. Chandler asked, turning from the board.

"Well, there's *cop-ro-lite*—"

"Ah, yes. Thank you. That's *fossilized* excrement, isn't it?" she asked, adding the word to the list.

"You *coprolite!*" someone said, trying the new word out for size.

"There's *flops* in here, too," said the girl with the thesaurus, causing another short burst of laughter.

"That's good, class. I think we've got them about covered now," Ms. Chandler said. "So let's see if we can classify some of these words. Mike, how would you handle this—"

"Well, personally, I wouldn't *handle* any of it—" Mike replied, while the class went bananas, especially cute little Mary Ann Olson.

Ms. Chandler, pretending she was not amused, began to write column headings on the board. SCIENTIFIC TERMS, she wrote, followed by VULGARITIES.

"Now there's an interesting word," she said, reaching for the dictionary on her desk and then flipping to the *V*'s. "Ah, here it is. '*Vulgar:* characteristic of or common to the great mass of people—' so forth and so forth," she said, skimming. "Okay, yes, this is what we're looking for—meaning number three: '*Vulgar:* characterized by a lack of culture, refinement, taste, restraint, sensitivity, etc.; coarse; crude; boorish'!" She looked up. "That's what *vulgar* means." She closed the dictionary and looked again at Mike. "Okay, Mike. So far we have *scientific terms* and *vulgarities*. Are there any other classifications?"

"There's baby talk—"

"All right," she said, adding BABY TALK. "Any others?"

"Slang?"

Ms. Chandler nodded and added SLANG to the column headings.

"How about, like, when it comes *just* from animals?" someone suggested.

"Good," Ms. Chandler agreed, quickly erasing her column headings and rewriting them in another order. "Now, let's classify."

And in a few moments the board looked like this:

SCIENTIFIC—HUMAN
- Excrement
- Feces
- Stool
- Manure
- Coprolite

SCIENTIFIC—ANIMAL
- Excrement
- Feces
- Stool
- Manure
- Coprolite
- Dung
- Scat
- Droppings
- Guano

VULGARITIES
- Shit
- Crap
- Turd

BABY TALK
- Number two
- Poop
- Ca-ca
- Doo-doo

SLANG
- Dingleberries
- Cow chips
- Cow pats
- Load
- Flops
- Business

"All right," said Ms. Chandler, checking her watch. "We may not have it exactly right in every case, but we don't have much time left. How many have noticed that although not every four-letter word is on the vulgarities list, *all* the vulgarities are four-letter words? Isn't that interesting! Other than that, though, what quality *makes* a word vulgar, and why is their use so prevalent today? Blue? You look like you may have something to say about that."

"Well, I don't know what makes a word vulgar. I don't know why *shit* is vulgar but *feces* isn't, but I think I *do* know why their use is so prevalent," said Blue with a sad, sweet smile. "It's because of the images they are meant to invoke. A long time ago my father told me that vulgar words are like weapons of the ill-mannered, meant to shock and disgust, something like changing a baby's smelly messy diaper on the table during dinner or picking snot from your nose and depositing the disgusting yellow globule on your plate for everyone to see."

Sounds of "Yuck!" and "Ech!" and "Gross!" suddenly filled the room. The images of a baby's messy diaper and plain old yellow snot had somehow become more shocking and disgusting to his classmates than the old familiar shit.

"But let's keep in mind our dictionary definition," said Ms. Chandler, winding up the lesson. "Perhaps, for those who lack culture, refinement, taste, restraint, and sensitivity, vulgar words have no effect." She smiled. "That may give us all something to think about. Class dismissed."

Mary Ann Olson hurriedly scooped up her books and barely managed to brush up against Mike as they squeezed through the doorway together.

It took only one Warriors game and two pizza dates before Mike discovered what a shallow character she really was.

In another one of those so-called coincidences of life—but which are, in reality, just events that happen to happen when they happen, and that if they *never* happened to happen when they happened, *that* would be *really* strange—Omaha received her invitation to Travis's wedding on the very same day that Blue would pass his driver's test. They were just "events," but one caused moping and sadness, and the other, exhilaration and joy.

Blue had already taken the written portion of his

driver's test and had scored 100 percent, but now he was required to actually prove his driving ability. Uncle Ralphy closed the barbershop a little early that Friday and was waiting in front of Blue's house when he came home from school. Of course, Blue was expecting to take his test in the stick-shift Chevy and was a bit surprised and slightly disappointed when he saw Uncle Ralphy sitting in that crazy Samwich Wagon instead. Even though Blue was happy to be taking the test, he thought that made-over van was the *ugliest* mode of transportation he had ever seen.

They took the long route to the motor vehicles office so Blue could get used to the clutch pedal and brake, and on the way over, Uncle Ralphy told him not once but several times to *listen carefully to your examiner, and do exactly as he says.*

Even though he had a four o'clock appointment, there were three men and a woman ahead of him in line, but finally his turn came up. Uncle Ralphy sat on the bench and gave him a nervous smile and the thumbs-up sign. "I'll wait for you here, Blue."

"All right," the examiner said, climbing in the passenger side while bending his neck and peering at the painted words *Wayne's Samwich Wagon* in a most dubious manner. "You may start your engine."

Blue started the engine, a souped-up Ford V-8 with dual carbs and a supercharger.

The examiner raised his eyebrows slightly at the sound and rolled up the window with a shake of his head. "Proceed ahead and stop on the painted yellow line."

Blue listened carefully to his examiner and did exactly as he said.

"Now put 'er in reverse and back up a couple of lengths."

"Lengths?" Blue ventured.

"Of cars. Of cars. Lengths of cars!"

"Okay. Yes, sir. I got it now."

"All right. Circle the parking lot and exit at the driveway on your left."

Circle the parking lot and exit at the driveway on my left.

"Proceed up this street until you come to the stoplight, and then turn right."

Proceed up this street until I come to the stoplight, and then turn right.

Blue had become a robot, doing exactly as he was told. A pedestrian crosswalk was between the driveway where he had turned left and the stoplight. Blue *did* see her there, the pedestrian, crossing slowly—her sensible shoes and black-strapped handbag. It wasn't that he didn't *see* her. It was just that he was hypnotized, a zombie waiting for instructions, waiting to hear the words: *Stop for the pedestrian.*

The examiner was filling out the boxes on the form—an *X* here, a check there. The instruction never came.

Blue's brain snapped to just in the nick of time. The pedestrian escaped unharmed, but Blue got five points off for the jerky stop.

An hour and fifteen minutes later, after standing in line for his photo and signing the proper forms, he pulled into Uncle Ralphy's driveway and parked in the spot by the fence. "I'm proud of you, my boy," Uncle Ralphy said. "And the Samwich Wagon is yours!"

Blue Avenger almost fainted. *"Mine?"* he exclaimed. "You mean, it's actually *mine?*"

And that is how a broken-down wreck with a rebuilt V-8 engine had suddenly turned into the most beautiful van in the world.

★ ★ ★

"Mom!" Omaha called out on that very same afternoon. "Look! I got a letter from Trav! And I think he actually wrote it himself!"

"Umm," Margie answered. "Look at that envelope. What a mess. What'd he do? Get the zip code wrong? And the house number, too! Look at the postmark. My God, that letter's been floating around for weeks!"

Omaha felt the anger rising in her chest. "Oh, Mom! He wrote it *himself!* Why can't you give him credit for trying? Jeez! Can't you *ever* say anything nice about him?"

"Sure," Margie answered, turning away. "If there was something nice to say, I'd be the first to say it."

Omaha tried to stop them, but the words seemed to have a mind of their own. "No, you wouldn't! You *wouldn't!* No wonder he turned out the way he did!"

Margie's face flushed, caused by a sudden rush of blood, caused in turn by a physiological change due to an emotional response. In other words, Margie was mad, and it showed in her face.

"When I need advice from you, my *dear*," Margie said, with sarcastic restraint, "I'll be sure to ask for it. I am *not* responsible for the situation in which Travis finds himself, and furthermore, I'll thank you to keep your—your *stupid* opinions to yourself!" Margie really meant to say *groundless*, but she couldn't think of the word just then.

Omaha bit her lip and turned her head so her mother wouldn't see her disgusted scowl. Then she tore open the envelope and started to read Trav's message. "Oh, God! He's getting married! He says he's met a girl through the want ads and they're getting *married!* Isn't that something! And there's more. Wait a minute." Omaha brought the scribbled piece of paper closer to her face and squinted. "Hey! He wants me to come! He wants me to be his—" Omaha broke off, laughing. "Isn't that just like him! He wrote that he wants me to be his 'best man,' then he crossed that out and wrote 'witness.' Then he put a big 'Ha ha.'" Omaha turned the paper over and looked at the other side, but there was nothing written there. "He—he didn't say anything about you, Mom."

"I'm not surprised." Margie checked her fingernails, scraping off a piece of old polish. "Well, when is it?"

"I'm just looking for that. Oh, *no!* It's *Sunday!* It's the day after tomorrow! That's the twelfth, isn't it?"

Omaha examined the postmark again. "He mailed it in plenty of time. It just took so long because of all these—" She almost said "mistakes," but then she didn't want to seem like she was criticizing Travis, so instead she asked, "Oh, Mom! How am I going to get there? How far is it to Walla Walla, anyway? You can drive us! I mean, you can still *come*. Just because he didn't mention—"

"Omaha, please don't talk foolish."

"What?"

"Don't talk foolish. You can't go all the way to Walla Walla."

"But I *want* to go! I haven't seen Travis since we moved away from Tulsa! I'm grown-up now and I want to see my brother!"

"I'm sorry. It's just out of the question. I have to work this weekend, and you have school—"

"Not on Sunday! God! Not on Saturday and Sunday!"

"It's hundreds of miles away," Margie said. "It's farther than Los Angeles, for heaven's sake. It's an overnight trip. So just forget it. You can send him a card. And besides, what sort of ding-a-ling would marry a guy—"

"Mom!" Omaha shouted. "Stop it! You have no right—" Knowing she was about to cry, Omaha quickly turned and went to her room, but she didn't slam the door. Omaha was not the door-slamming type.

She sat down on the edge of her bed and tried to think of what to do. Her first thought—*Greyhound*. That was it! She could take the bus! The phone was in the kitchen, and so was Margie. Undaunted, Omaha looked up the number and dialed. They kept her on hold for several minutes, playing music and telling her what a wonderful trip she was going to have on Greyhound, and finally a real person came on the line.

Omaha spoke right up. "Can you give me some information about—uh, I mean, I want to get from here to Walla Walla, Washington, and—yes, that's right—"

Margie stopped what she was doing and just stared and stared at Omaha as if she were seeing her for the very first time. And in a way, she was. She was seeing a young woman with a mind of her own, who was going to do what she wanted.

"Yes?" Omaha said brightly. Then, "Oh. Three forty in the afternoon, arrives four fifteen the *next day?* You mean, if I went tomorrow at three forty, I wouldn't get there until four fifteen on Sunday? *That* long? And there's no way—Oh. I see. Yes. Well, thank you." Omaha hung up the phone and looked Margie straight in the eye. "I thought I could take the bus, but it's too late for that." Omaha went back to her room, realizing that her mother was her last hope now but knowing that her chances were very slim indeed. She had to rehearse her request with care.

Margie had the radio on in the kitchen, so Omaha didn't hear the doorbell, but at seventeen minutes after six Margie rapped on her bedroom door with a short warning knock, poked her head in, and announced, "That strange redheaded kid is here. He says he has something to show you."

"Blue? Do you mean Blue?" Omaha got up from her bed. "Where is he? Did you invite him in?"

"Well, sort of. But he's still on the porch."

What Blue had to show her, of course, was Wayne's Samwich Wagon, the most beautiful van in the world. But as much as she wanted to and as hard as she tried, Omaha could just not bring herself to tell Blue about Trav.

eleven

But three hours and ten minutes later, she could. Although Margie seemed to have grown a bit more sympathetic to Omaha's appeal, she still declined the invitation to drive her to Walla Walla. Blue Avenger was her final hope. So at twenty-seven minutes after nine that Friday evening, Omaha went back to the kitchen and picked up the phone once more.

Blue answered on the first ring. "Hello," he said.

Omaha put her lips close to the mouthpiece. "Scotu! M-sot! Fiotu!" she said softly.

"Omaha?" he asked, after just a slight pause.

"I need your help, and I need it badly. I want you to take me to Walla Walla, Washington, tomorrow in Wayne's Samwich Wagon. I have a half brother I never told you about who is incarcerated there, and he's getting married on Sunday morning. He wants me to be his best man. That is, he wants me to be his witness. And Blue, I really, *really* want to go." (There! It was out. Part one of her dreadful secret was out, but telling part two would be murder.)

Blue Avenger swallowed hard. "Omaha," he said, "I believe that is a request which requires permission from a higher authority. And from *your* mother also, I would think. I will pick you and your mother up in fifteen minutes, and we will come over here and thrash it out together."

Thirty minutes later, after Josh had been sent to get ready for bed, the four of them—Sally, Margie, Omaha, and Blue—were sitting around the cozy table in Blue's kitchen. It was, by far, the most difficult decision that Sally Schumacher ever had to make concerning her son. And she didn't make it lightly. In the end, it was Omaha's heartrending entreaties and Blue's trustworthiness that eventually swung the deal. Josh would have to accompany them, of course, and they would leave as early as possible the next morning. In a few minutes, when she got home, Margie would call and reserve two rooms for the following night at a Walla Walla motel, which she would charge on her Visa—a magnanimous gesture motivated by guilt, but which, nevertheless, caused Omaha's eyebrows to raise up nineteen millimeters in the vast majority of countries in the world but three-quarters of an inch (give or take a smidgen) in the

U.S. of A. The gas for the trip would be paid for by Omaha from her weekly allowance, and even though she volunteered to buy the meals as well, Sally quickly vetoed that idea, calling it "unnecessary." They would head for home directly after the wedding, and the estimated arrival time back in Oakland would be very late Sunday night—more likely, the wee hours of Monday morning, and they would all attend school the next day as usual. Blue would obey all traffic laws, and (this with a stern look from Margie) there would be absolutely no hanky-panky *whatsoever*.

"What's hanky-panty?" asked Josh, who had returned to the kitchen just in time to mishear the phrase. "Is it like—" he began, laughing and holding on to his stomach in a typical ten-year-old bout of silly, senseless shenanigans. "Is it blowing your nose on your panties? Ha ha ha ha!" he laughed, falling to the floor— a little shtick that Margie pretended to ignore.

"Oh, jeez," Blue breathed in Omaha's ear. "This could have been such a wonderful trip."

At ten minutes after eight the next morning, Blue and Josh pulled up in front of Omaha's house in Wayne's

Samwich Wagon, which was all gassed up and ready to go. Moments before, Omaha had picked up the morning *Star* from under the bushes, tossed it into the house, and slammed shut the door. Now she was waiting on the porch, dressed in jeans and a dark blue sweater and carrying an overnight bag, a black binder scrapbook of newspaper clippings, a thin plastic sack containing three ham sandwiches and six apples, and two road maps—since they had agreed the night before that she would be their navigator. A nice beige coat was draped over one arm.

Blue, wearing his vest and kaffiyeh—since this *was* a business trip—jumped out and put her overnight bag and coat into the back part of the van as she climbed up on the front seat beside Josh with her binder, the food, and the maps. Then Blue went back around to his side, climbed in, and started the engine.

"Hi," Omaha said, putting her junk on the floor between her feet.

"Hi," said Josh.

"Hi," said Blue. "So, which way?"

"Head east on 80 and turn north on 505, just past Vacaville. I'll tell you when."

"Right."

"Then we're taking 5, on past Redding and Weed, to Highway 97, where we go, go, go, past Klamath Falls and Bend and Biggs, all the way to Highway 84 east and on to Pendleton, where we turn north again on Highway 11, and right on up to Walla Walla."

Blue hesitated. "Right," he said finally. "But you didn't even *look* at the map."

"No sweat, Blue. I checked it last night. Don't worry. I'll tell you when to turn. And I just called for a weather and road report," she added. "The weekend forecast is 'clear,' and all the roads are open."

"Sounds good. Let's go!"

No one spoke for several minutes. The whole thing was just too exciting for words.

It was Josh who broke the silence—with a question intended to be funny. "Are we there yet, Mommy?" he asked in a whiny little-boy voice.

But Omaha was more than ready to play *that* game. "Pipe down, you stupid little brat," she answered quickly, "or I'll kick your butt from here to Biggs!" The look of surprise and horror on Josh's face was so hilarious that Blue almost had to pull over to the side, he was laughing so hard.

Josh caught on in a second, of course, and even blushed at his own gullibility.

Omaha impulsively brought her hand up to the back of his head and rumpled his hair. "Scared you, huh!" she said with a grin.

"Nah," he answered, beginning to scratch his arm—for Josh Schumacher had just been bitten by a small black dipterous fly known to entomologists as *Plecia nearctica*, but more commonly called the lovebug.

(An interesting but unfinished study was once undertaken by a second-year graduate student and amateur gymnast at the University of Wisconsin, who subsequently shocked her friends and family by dropping out of the English program and joining the circus. Had she persisted in her research, she would have discovered that only 1.3 percent of all readers habitually stop to look up words they don't know. For the information of the remaining 98.7 percent, dipterous means "having two wings, as some insects, or two winglike appendages, as some seeds.")

Because they had to leave so early that morning, neither Josh nor Omaha nor Blue had time to read the day's

"Ask Auntie Annie." But just because they didn't read it doesn't mean it wasn't there. And this is what it said:

ASK AUNTIE ANNIE, by Annie Marzipan

Dear Readers: You are SO wonderful! I simply knew I could count on you, my wonderful faithful readers!

When I asked for your weepless meringue recipes, your response was tremendous! I received a total of 7,396 letters, each one with a recipe for weepless meringue! As you might imagine, my devoted assistants have been very busy testing those recipes, and I have bad news and good news: The bad news is that 7,395 of your recipes failed miserably. The good news is that one did not! A recipe sent in by a mysterious someone called Blue Avenger from Oakland, California, did the trick! Unfortunately Blue Avenger did not include his (or her) telephone number, so I could not personally thank him (or her) for his (or her) marvelous, wonderful breakthrough recipe. Mr. Chase R. Wanner, president of the Wanner Cornstarch Company, can't wait to print Blue Avenger's recipe on the side of each and every cornstarch box, which he will do just as soon as humanly possible. And as promised, Mr. Wanner is sending a gift of appreciation to Blue Avenger: a lifetime supply of Wanner Cornstarch! Happy baking, Blue Avenger!

So, my faithful readers, BE SURE to read this column in tomorrow's edition, when I will print Blue Avenger's exclusive recipe just for you! THE LAST MERINGUE—BLUE AVENGER'S WEEPLESS WONDER LEMON MERINGUE PIE.

Note to local editors: Please save a little extra space for me tomorrow. If you love lemon meringue pie (and who doesn't?), you won't regret it!

". . . sixty-four bottles of beer. If one of those bottles should happen to fall, sixty-three bottles of beer on the wall. Sixty-three bottles of beer on the wall, sixty-three bottles of beer. If one of those bottles should happen to fall, sixty-two bottles of beer on the wall. Sixty-two bottles of beer on the wall, sixty-two bottles of beer. If one of those—"

"Joshy, did you know there just might be a big meat grinder in perfect running order sitting right there on a shelf in the back of this van?"

*". . . bottles should happen—*no, I didn't—*to fall, sixty-one bottles of—"*

"Josh, how would you like to be made into a human samwich? Would you like that? And tell me this: After you are ground up into zillions of little pieces, would you prefer to be smathered over with mayonnaise or mustard?"

". . . *beer on the*—smathered? What's that?—*Sixty bottles of*—"

"I think what Blue is trying to tell you, Josh, honey, is that maybe you'd better can the singing for a while, even though I, personally, find it *most* entertaining."

"Okay. Whatever you say, Omaha."

For the following ten seconds, there was only the sound of the purring of the V-8 engine and the gentle, relieved sighs of two of the occupants in the front enclosed area of Wayne's Samwich Wagon.

"Hey, Omaha," Josh said, "I'm still hungry. Do we have anything else to eat?"

"Sorry, no. The apples and samwiches; that's all I brought. Maybe we can stop in a little while."

"Omaha?"

"Yes, Josh?"

"Would you please tell my brother—that character next to me with the stupid blue towel wrapped around his head—that someone in this van has to go to the bathroom really *bad?*"

"Certainly. I would be more than honored. Ahem. Blue?"

"Yes, my love?"

"I heard that!" Josh exclaimed, bolting upright in his seat. "And I'm going to tell! Omaha's mother said no *hanky-panty!*"

"Aha!" said the one with the towel. "Obviously you have forgotten your own definition! Do you see me blowing my nose on my panty? No, you don't! So just *what* are you going to tell?"

One lone sigh. Then, *"—Sixty bottles of beer on the wall, sixty bottles of beer—"*

Blue stopped for fuel just north of Redding. They had been on the road for three hours and thirty-three minutes, and so far they had not spoken one word about Travis. After they gassed up Wayne, they left him parked in the lot while they walked the short distance over to Rusty's Hamburger Joynt.

Omaha had placed their order and was already seated in a corner booth by the window when Josh emerged from the rest room and quickly slid in beside her. When Blue came out, he was obliged to sit opposite them, and in a moment, when their number was called, he went to the counter and picked up their food.

"Boy, am I starved!" Josh said, taking a huge bite of

his hamburger. "Is this supposed to be our lunch or what?"

"Please don't talk with your mouth full, Josh," Blue said. "It is very disgusting."

"Oops, sorry!" Josh said, tucking an errant piece of lettuce into his mouth and quickly glancing at Omaha, whom he certainly didn't wish to offend.

"So, why are we doing this, anyway?" Josh asked, after making a point of swallowing every last morsel.

"Because we're hungry, I guess—" Blue said, noting the sudden troubled look on Omaha's brow and trying his best to mitigate the question.

"No! I don't mean that! I mean, why—ouch!"

"I'm invited to my brother's wedding, Josh," Omaha began. "Actually, he's really my half brother—"

"Oh, yeah? Which half? Yuk yuk."

"Please be quiet, Josh, and let her explain," Blue said, with controlled politeness.

"He happens to be in jail," Omaha continued, "and I haven't seen him for five years."

"Do you ever talk on the phone?" Blue asked gently. "Are prison—I mean, are they allowed to make phone calls from—that is—"

Omaha reached across the table and put her hand on Blue's arm. "Do you mean, are prisoners allowed to make phone calls from the jail? Yes, they are. But—oh, you won't believe this, it's just so *hard* to believe, that a person's own *mother* could—well, anyway, we've always had an unlisted phone number. My mother told me once it was because of her work, that she didn't want to be listed in the phone book because sometimes people think nurses may have drugs lying around the house. Can you believe that! God, what a lie that was! Because the real reason we've had an unlisted number all this time is because she didn't want Travis calling us up! And she is his *mother!*"

It was too much for Omaha. She quickly wiped her eyes with the back of her hand and put her head down on the yellow Formica table.

"What's he in for, anyway?" Josh asked, being only ten years old and not yet attuned to the subtle sensitivities of others—a trait that is not always guaranteed to come with age. "Ouch! Will you quit kicking me, David!"

Omaha raised her head. "He's in for murder, Josh," she said, speaking his name but looking directly into Blue Avenger's eyes. "He was just twenty years old, and he shot another man dead."

"*Really!* Wow!"

Blue crumpled up his hamburger wrapper and stuffed it into his plastic cup. "Let's hit the road, you guys. We've got a long ways yet to go."

Omaha opened her scrapbook just after Chemult and before La Pine on Highway 97. "It wasn't his fault," she was saying. "Because, don't you see, nothing is *ever* anyone's fault."

Joshua Schumacher perked up his ears. "Hold it," he said. "Did you say *nothing is ever anyone's fault?* Do you mean I can do anything I want, and it won't be my fault?"

Omaha sighed and shook her head. "Oh, God! Why does it always come to this? That's the first thing people say. *I can do anything I want, and it won't be my fault.* Why don't they ever say, *I won't take credit for the good I do and I won't blame others for the bad they do?* Oh"—she sighed—"I don't know. Life is just too crazy. Who can figure it out?" She leaned her forehead against the glass and stared despondently out the window.

Blue checked the rearview mirror. There wasn't another car in sight. He really didn't want to upset

Omaha any further, but there was something he had to say. "I just have one problem with all that," he began, glancing her way to see how she would react.

Omaha turned and looked at him. "With what?" She brushed the back of her hand across her nose and sniffed a couple of times in quick succession.

"With your no-fault theory," he answered. He forced a little laugh. "God, it sounds like an insurance policy."

Omaha was not amused. "Go on," she said. "What's your problem with it?"

"Well, I don't think you can excuse *everything*—every rotten thing a person does"—he snapped his fingers—"just like that! I mean—" Blue faltered, not sure how to put his thoughts into words.

Omaha stared at him. "Go on," she challenged.

"Okay, well, take serial killers, for instance. No." He paused. "Take Hitler. Take Adolf Hitler! Now there's a good example for you. Here's a guy who was responsible for the deaths—the torture and deaths of millions of people—Jews, homosexuals, Gypsies, political dissidents. Millions of people, Omaha! To say that wasn't his fault, well, I can't go along with that."

"Well, that's just tough, Blue!" Omaha said so

loudly that Josh sat up with a jerk. "Hitler was a crazy maniac, for God's sake! He was not a sane human being! And neither were all those other people around him who let all that Holocaust stuff happen! Why does everybody always have to *blame* somebody? I'll bet you a million dollars that if you opened up those brains, Hitler's brain, Goerbel's brain, or whatever that guy's name was, you'd find some kind of abnormality there. *It is not normal to kill millions of people, Blue!* And all those civilians who stood by and let it happen, there was something wrong with them, too! It must be something like a virus, people's brains can become sort of infected—like from mass hysteria or something. Whatever it was, it was *something!* And I think that if they could have done something about it, they would have!"

Blue was genuinely surprised at the degree of her agitation. "Well, I don't know," he said finally. "I just can't excuse it. How can you *not* hold people responsible for atrocities like that?" He shook his head. "I just don't know."

Omaha sighed deeply. "Okay, Blue, answer me this," she said quietly. "Why did some people resist? You know, resist Hitler and that fascist stuff? What *made*

191

them resist? What did they have that the others didn't have? How did they get it? Did they just say to themselves, 'I'm going to do the right thing'? Something *made* them do the right thing! Don't you see?" Omaha shut her eyes and let her head drop to her chest. "I'm getting a headache. Can we continue this later?"

"Well, hey," Josh suggested gently, happy to change the subject, "what were you going to read to us?" He reached over and turned a page of her scrapbook. "What are all these—these clippings or articles or whatever they are?"

Omaha shifted over in her seat, making more room for Josh to turn the pages. But she continued to stare out the window.

Josh leaned forward, studying the scrapbook, finally pulling it onto his own lap—all the while stealing crossways glances at Omaha, watching her eyes become shiny with tears.

"This one looks interesting," Josh said with false cheeriness.

NEW STUDIES LEND SUPPORT TO "ALCOHOLISM GENE" FINDING

"So what's that about, Omaha? Why did you clip this one out?"

Omaha only shook her head again and shielded her left eye with her hand, surreptitiously wiping away a little tear of frustration.

"What does 'pre-dis-pose' mean?" Josh went on. "It says here they think they've discovered a gene that may pre-dis-pose people to alcoholism and other mental health problems, like drug abuse and other stuff. Hey! This is *really* interesting!" He paused. "Omaha? Are you okay? Omaha, watch this." Josh took her hand, the one that was shielding her eye, and placed it back in her lap. Then he grabbed his left thumb in the palm of his right hand and bent it all the way back to his wrist. "Can you do that? Can you do that, Omaha?"

Getting no response from her, Josh again directed his attention to the scrapbook on his lap.

WHAT MAKES FOR
A SUNNY DISPOSITION
Left Frontal Brain Activity Is
Happier Brain Activity

" 'People with more activity in their left frontal cortex than in their right one seem to be of a more cheerful tem-per-a-ment than others,' " he read. "Hey, Omaha," he said, giving her a little nudge. "How's that left frontal cortex of yours doing? Not too good, huh?"

There was just a flicker of a response. Encouraged, he suddenly exclaimed, "Omaha! Omaha! Watch this! Look!" He stuck out his tongue and made it curl up along the edges into a long, tubular shape. "David can't even do that, can you, David? Look, David. Can you do this?" Josh repeated the thing with his tongue, this time wiggling it around a bit.

"I'm trying to drive, Josh. Okay?"

"You mean like this?" Omaha said, for Josh's antics were so touching and cute.

Josh laughed uproariously. "Good! That's good!"

"Okay, okay. Give me back the scrapbook," Omaha said, resigned. "I'll read a couple of these to you guys, but it's just going to start this argument up all over again."

GOOD GRAMMAR LINKED TO GOOD GENES, STUDIES SUGGEST

" 'Surprising hints are turning up that suggest people may inherit their ability to use language well,' " she read. "And then the article goes on to tell about some studies in Canada on a group of people who have no ability to conjugate verbs and that it apparently runs in families. Here's another article on the same study, only in a lighter vein:

TRY USING THIS EXCUSE ON YOUR ENGLISH TEACHER

"Yes, this is the same study," she said, turning the page. "Here's one, something like that other one Josh read about alcoholism:

ODDS ARE, GAMBLING URGE IS JUST CHEMISTRY, STUDY SAYS

"Let's see. The big thing here is that 'gamblers and alcoholics share similar biological traits' and that 'compulsive gamblers may have below normal levels of serotonin, a substance needed for brain cells to communicate.' "

Omaha turned another page. "But do you guys see what I'm getting at?" she asked. "Don't you see how all these articles tell about—well, like I was just saying—they all seem to be saying the same thing, and that is that people really *can't* help how they are or what they do. It's in their genes or their chemicals." Omaha paused a moment, slowly turning the pages of her scrapbook. "Here's another:

BRAIN-CELL CLUE TO HOMOSEXUALITY
2 Studies Find Tissue Differences
Between Gay and Straight Men

"And here's one I find of special interest," Omaha said finally. "Listen to this:

METAL FOUND IN CRIMINALS' HAIR
High Levels in Convicts May Indicate
Metabolic Disorder

" 'The level of manganese found in the hair of convicted criminals is significantly higher than in other members of society,' say brain researchers at the University of

California, Irvine. 'This could mean that such prisoners are suffering from a metabolic disorder that affects the brain.' "

Omaha looked up from her scrapbook and glanced quickly from Blue to Josh and then to Blue again. "See there!" she exclaimed. "See? If these prisoners have this—this disorder, and it shows up like that, with that manganese in their hair, well, don't you see? It means that they're *different*, somehow. And it's not their fault that they're in jail! It's *not!*"

Blue reached over Josh's head and grasped Omaha's shoulder, still keeping his eyes on the road, which was quite heavy with traffic now. "I know," he said. "I know." And then he reached up and touched her cheek and smoothed her hair.

After a few moments Josh grabbed Blue's forearm and, ducking his head, raised it up and over, placing his brother's hand back on the steering wheel. "No hanky-panty, remember?" he said. "Just drive, David. Drive."

The subject came up again after they had stopped at Biggs and were once again on the road. "My turn in the middle," Omaha had said as they climbed back into the van, and a few minutes later Josh was asleep, with his head resting against her shoulder and his mouth pulled slightly ajar.

"Well, I have to admit, it does explain a lot," Blue started, speaking softly so as not to wake the kid. "That no-fault theory of yours. It explains it all, the misery and cruelty, the suffering, the sheer lunacy of life, this tale told by an idiot—"

"The fishing vest and the towel, too?" Omaha added with a smile. "And guns and wars and deluded hordes of football fans—believing in transmitted glory?"

That took Blue's breath away, that final thought of hers. How could it be that they were so alike?

A flock of birds swooped low directly in their line of vision and then circled to the left, not a single one leaving the group. "They're doing what they have to do," Omaha said with a sigh. "Just like the rest of us, you know."

Blue had been driving since ten after eight that morning, except for the times they had stopped, and now his eyes were scratchy and red, and his legs and feet felt like lead. "Do you think it might be a matter of degrees?" he asked. "I mean, that part of us we think of as 'I,' does it make any decisions at *all?*"

"I don't see how it could," she said. "And I've thought about that a lot."

"But there, you see?" he said. "You made *that* decision, after all—"

"Ah, Blue," she said with a quiet smile. "See what a trap we're in? We're so used to *thinking* we make decisions, but it's just the way we think. Our brains sift through all the stuff up there, our genes, our experiences, our memories, what we had for breakfast, all turned to chemicals now. Then our brains hand us their conclusions, right there on a platter. We think what we think, and we do what we do, and we think we did it all ourselves."

"What?" Blue laughed gently.

And she laughed, too.

"So, why do we bother with all this?" he said after a while.

"With all what?"

"With life, with living. Once we realize we're just like robots, acting out our parts—"

"Because we have to, I guess. Maybe we're programmed to be curious, to see what we'll do next, and waiting to see what will *happen* to us next."

Neither of them spoke for a while. Omaha shifted slightly in her seat, adjusting Josh's head on her shoulder. "Look at him sleep. He's really a good little kid."

Blue glanced at his brother and feigned a scowl. "Little monster, you mean," he said, and Omaha smiled. "But you know," Blue said, continuing their conversation, "it's funny you said that, about waiting to see what will happen to us next, because I've been thinking about that, too. We talk about having free will in making choices, but life is made up of more than simply making choices, isn't it? First we have to have these choices given to us. And that's the part we definitely can't help. That part is already determined for us. Call it luck or fate or whatever you want. But most of the things that happen in our lives are in this category, I think. They just *happen*. Conscious choice has nothing to do with it. Free will doesn't even enter into the picture—yet."

"Yeah." Omaha nodded. "That's right."

"Well, I'm just trying to clear this up in my own mind. I'm probably repeating myself, but I can't help it. So here we are, presented with certain choices. And actually, like I said, I think our lives may depend more on what *happens* to us than what choices we make, or *think* we make," he added with an acknowledging smile in her direction.

"Really?"

"Well, sure. Look at us, for instance. How come we met? We didn't *choose* to meet. I was already living here, going to San Pablo High, minding my own business, and you just happened to move here. See? Pure chance."

Omaha smiled, just a small hint of a smile. And Blue looked at her and smiled back.

"But the big question still remains—for me, at least," he said. "Once we are presented with choices, are we free to choose or not? This is really starting to bug me!" he added, pounding the steering wheel with his fist, a gesture totally out of character for him.

Omaha let the question hang in the air for a moment. Then she touched his arm. "Blue, do you remember that day you changed your name, when we were walking out by the barracks—and you told me you loved me?"

Blue, surprised by the question, surprised she would mention that now, answered the only way he could. "I'll *never* forget that." Then, to lighten the moment, he added, "Does a guy ever forget the first time he tells a girl he loves her? Not likely!"

But Omaha was deadly serious. "So, I guess that means you would do anything for me? Isn't that part of what love means?"

Blue sensed a trap. "No," he said slowly. "There are some things I wouldn't do, even for you. For instance, I wouldn't kill for you. Remember those kids in the news? The girl asked the guy to kill one of his old girlfriends, and he did? I wouldn't do that for you." Glancing at her briefly, he paused and said, "But then, you'd never ask me to do something like that."

"So, that proves you have free will, right? You could *choose* not to kill for me."

Blue felt the noose tightening. "Well, yes. Maybe. I'm not sure. Maybe, to take a leaf out of your book, maybe I just don't have it *in* me to kill. Maybe I couldn't kill anyone even if I thought I wanted to. But yes, for the sake of argument, let's say I made that choice freely. That it was a real choice."

Omaha touched his arm again. Then she leaned over as far as she could without disturbing the sleeping Josh and whispered in his ear, "What if I told you what I *really* wanted was for you to stop loving me? You have free will. Could you stop loving me, if that was what I really wanted?"

Blue felt a little shiver run through his body. What kind of dumb, blind luck sent a girl like this into his life?

twelve

Wayne's Samwich Wagon pulled into the small parking lot of the Red Onion Motel in Walla Walla, Washington, at ten minutes after two in the morning. Blue was the only person still awake in the van.

"Okay, gang, we're here," he said, closing his eyes at last and letting his forehead fall to the steering wheel with a clunk.

They had to ring the bell to wake the manager, who signed them in and gave them two keys—room 109 and room 111. "Checkout time is twelve noon sharp," he said dully, "and there's free coffee and doughnuts in the office until nine. Good night and pleasant dreams."

"Oh, excuse me, sir?" Omaha asked. "How far is it to the—uh, the prison?"

"Just five blocks up that way"—he pointed, accustomed to the question—"and then eight blocks to your right. Good night again and pleasant dreams."

Blue Avenger may be the unlikely hero of San Pablo High, but he is also human. Once Josh was in the sack, in just three minutes flat, Blue stepped out of room 109 and quietly tapped shave-and-a-haircut with his finger-nail on the unscreened window of room 111. The curtain moved, and moved again, and Omaha opened the door.

The room was stuffy and smelled of cigarettes. It was lit only by a 25-watt bulb in a two-tone beige ceramic lamp topped with a pleated shade standing alongside a black telephone on an imitation wooden dresser backed by a rectangle-shaped mirror. In a small alcove at the rear of the room was a sink with a white plastic drain-board on either side, a large wavy mirror in back of it, and a hand towel and washcloth tightly folded in a chrome towel rack on the wall. A dark green wool dress and Omaha's coat were barely visible hanging in another alcove to the left of the sink, and on the floor was a pair of high-heel shoes, the color of which exactly matched the dress. Omaha's overnight case was lying open on the bed. A television set was hanging in a seemingly precar-ious but perfectly safe angle from the wall. It was not turned on. A very large colorful print of an impression-istic French street scene was hanging in a nicked wooden frame above the bed. One large upholstered chair, worn and lopsided, was placed in the corner by the window.

"I thought I'd better check—just to see if you were all right, of course," Blue said, almost in a whisper, since it was after two o'clock in the morning. What a marvelous, wonderfully funny thing to say! Omaha thought, smiling inwardly so as not to spoil the subtlety of the joke.

They were still standing in the small space between the door and the bed. Blue had taken off his blue towel and vest and was now dressed in just a regular long-sleeved shirt and jeans. They were very close to each other, but not yet touching.

It is impossible to say which of them made the first move, for, in fact, it was a simultaneous action. They stood together with their arms around each other for a very long time because they had waited so long and because it was so wonderful. And the kiss, when it happened, was nothing like in the movies. There was no desperate openmouthed urgency, no rapid movement from lips to throat to other places and back up again to the lips—the kind of kiss that, when it occurs in the movies, causes the women in the audience to slip down further in their seats and turn their heads ever so slightly to see how their date is taking it, while the men breathe deeply and try to pretend that it's all old stuff to them.

"Oh, Blue, my darling," Omaha whispered after the sweet, soft merging of their lips was over and her head was once again resting on his chest, "it was thoughtful of you to think of checking on me, because I was frightened, you know, all alone in this little motel room—"

What a marvelous, wonderfully funny thing to say! Blue thought, smiling inwardly so as not to spoil the subtlety of the joke. He took her by the hand and led her the two short steps to the lopsided chair, where he sat down ever so gracefully and gently maneuvered her onto his lap.

"You didn't believe me, did you?" Blue asked, after he had traced his forefinger down from her forehead, over her nose and lips and down her neck to a point right above her thyroid, a large ductless gland that was blithely going about its business secreting thyroxin, a hormone that regulates body growth and metabolism.

Omaha took hold of the hand with the trailing finger and kissed it. "When?" she asked with a perplexed look, since she couldn't remember ever not believing him.

Blue paused, giving her a chance to think. "When I told you we'd be alone together in a motel before you knew it," he said triumphantly.

Omaha was momentarily taken aback. She sat up straight and cocked her head, staring off toward the wall. "My God! Now *that* is spooky!"

Blue laughed and held up his hands. "Just a fluke, a stroke of luck, I promise—" he said. "You *know* I didn't plan *this*."

After another kiss, or two or three—it is difficult to say precisely, since it was not too clear when one stopped and another began—but after a while, Blue stopped the kissing and sighed a deep and thoughtful sigh.

What a tangled mess they were in! What a confusion of arms and legs and hormones and thoughts—a beating of hearts and age-old longings, a rush of memories, a clash of neurons, a snatch of a song. Was it cause or design, this mystery of life? Did anyone know? *Could* anyone know?

"You know something, Blue?" Omaha asked in the long, pregnant pause that followed.

"What?" whispered Blue, his lips on her hair.

"Well, I've always thought it would be sort of nice if—" Omaha faltered, suddenly overtaken by a wave of unaccustomed shyness.

"Yes?" Blue urged gently. "Go on. Nice if what?"

"Well, I've always thought," she started again, "that it would be really *nice*, you know, since sex is so—well—so *special*, wouldn't it be lovely if—" She blushed and hesitated again in the faint glow of the 25-watt bulb, because the concept was so new and wonderful and she had to search for the words. "—Wouldn't it be lovely if people could *wait*, until they were really *sure*, and then maybe there could be just *one*—"

Oh, Omaha, my Omaha, his heart began to sing, for the idea—so novel and strange—had also occurred to him!

They slowly rose from the chair and shared one last lingering kiss. "I'll think of you all through the night, and see you in the morning," Blue whispered as she quietly let him out the door.

Impossible and far-fetched? Could never happen in a million years? Probably so. Except for one thing: It did.

"You made it! You made it!" Travis exclaimed, rushing up to the girl in the dark green wool dress. "My God, how you've grown! But still you look the same!"

"Oh, Trav!" she said as they clasped hands and hugged and kissed each other's cheeks.

"You didn't call me," he said, with a hint of a pout. "So I wasn't sure you'd make it."

"No, I really wasn't sure myself—until just yesterday," she answered with a tremor in her voice. "And I didn't *know* I could call you. Mom never said I could call. So do you have a phone in your—your cell, or what?"

"Oh, no," he said, "we don't have phones in our rooms, but they do take messages for us, if they think they're on the up-and-up, and then we can make outgoing calls. But *your* mother doesn't want me calling," he said bitterly. "So she can just go—"

"No, Trav! No! Let's not talk about her! It's just so good to see you, let's not spoil it by—"

"Ah, there's my little bride now!" Travis said suddenly, looking past Omaha's shoulder to the visitors' entrance. "There's my little Peachie Pie!"

The next few moments were a happy blur, a maze of conversation and half introductions.

"—and Josh, you say? Well, put 'er there, Josh! It's nice to know you, pal."

"—and my friend, Blue, who drove me here—"

"—my name is Dalton Winger—I'm an inmate here, and this is my brother, Roger. He's quite a genius, you know. I share a room with Trav. Where did you say you were from? Now is *this* a happy day?"

"—Peaches Calhoun, my bride!"

"—no, I'm just a friend. I drove her here—"

"—yes, I'm to do the honors. A nondenominational service, but you can call me Preach." The tall man in the brown suit looked around at the group. "I think we'd better get started, folks," he said. "Peaches and Travis, will you stand here, please—"

Blue and Omaha held hands during the short ceremony while Josh, bored with it all, kept glancing around the room at the prisoners and their guests, who were seated at tables and talking quietly among themselves, and Josh couldn't tell which was which. In a corner of the room several small children were sitting on the floor in a trance, watching the television.

When it was over, Travis, Peaches, and Omaha, with tears in their eyes, formed a little family group, not meaning to exclude the others, but essentially that is the way it happened.

Josh wandered off to watch the television and the Preach went home, while Blue and the Winger brothers sat down together at a nearby vacant table.

And that is how Blue happened to be among the first to hear about the soon-to-be-famous Winger Stinger, the hands-down totally revolutionary invention of the century.

"Could we please stop for some food before we get *all* the way home?" implored Josh with a frown. "My stomach is starting to roar!"

They had been on the road for almost an hour, and they were all enmeshed in their own private thoughts.

"Okay, okay," said Blue. "The next place we see, we'll stop."

"I liked her a lot, didn't you?" said Omaha, who didn't feel hungry at all. "Did you see the way they looked at each other? Trav told me it was a case of love at first sight, for both of them."

"Pure genius," mused Blue, as he was beginning to formulate his plan for addressing the Oakland City Council. "A tranquilizing bullet that self-adjusts to fit any muzzle." He nudged Omaha with his shoulder.

"Did I tell you about that solution? You know, the tranquilizing solution?"

Omaha shook her head. "No. I don't think so."

"Well, the Winger brothers have been working with these veterinary researchers for years, at UC Davis or somewhere, and they've finally come up with this new tranquilizing agent. It's instantaneous, but it doesn't really put you out or anything. I mean, you're not knocked out cold. It just affects your muscles, and you can't move or talk for at least an hour. Like for self-defense, or if someone breaks into your house or something—it's perfect!"

"Well, that sounds great," Omaha said with a yawn. "But what I don't understand is why Peaches's family wouldn't even come to the wedding! They could at least support her that much!"

"I think I'd like a burger and fries," said Josh, rubbing his ten-year-old tummy.

"*Guns don't kill people* is how I'll start. That should get their attention."

"—or maybe a blueberry waffle, loaded with whipped cream."

"Trav told me they'll have to *wait their turn* to spend

the night together. They have a trailer for that, you know. Oh, how hard that must be for them to wait! And then they can only use it once a month—"

"Guns don't kill people, *but bullets do!*"

"No, maybe a plate of fried chicken, with onion rings on the side. Hey, there's a place! There's a place!" shouted Josh. "That coffee shop, there on the right!"

The booths were all taken, so they sat three in a row at the counter and they all ordered burgers and fries.

"And I learned something interesting about my father," Omaha was saying to Blue. "Trav solved part of that old mystery about *George or Don Broomo.* Remember I told you about that?"

Blue nodded, at the same time snatching Josh's straw before he had a chance to blow the wrapper toward the waitress's back. "Oh, yes. George or Don Broomo. So who are they, then, and what does it mean?"

"It's something like that old Adaman Eve thing." She smiled. "George or Don Broomo is Giordano Bruno! It just *sounded* like George or Don Broomo to me. He's the guy who had the guts to stand up for what he believed, remember? The guy they burned at the stake. My father had a real obsession about that guy. That's how he is," she added wistfully. "He used to get so intense sometimes. He would get all wound up in something and it would sort of take over. That's all he'd talk about. It drove my mother crazy."

Blue nodded. "Yeah. I've known people like that—"

"But I still don't understand how my father could visit him," Omaha continued. "Because that's what he would tell my mother. He had to go every year and see old George or Don Broomo. But he's been dead for centuries. How could he go over there and see him?" Omaha paused and looked off into space. "You know, I wonder, though. Did my father really pursue his dream, like he said he was going to do? I just wonder if he did." She turned and looked at Blue again. "Do you suppose he ever thinks of me?" Her voice began to break. "Oh, Blue, I know I said that I sometimes think our lives are all planned out. But does that mean I can never find him? Does that mean we will *never* meet again, no matter what I do?"

Meanwhile, unbeknownst to Blue Avenger, he was getting more and more famous with each passing hour:

ASK AUNTIE ANNIE, by Annie Marzipan

Dear Readers: As I promised yesterday, here is that marvelous recipe from Blue Avenger, of Oakland, California, *exactly* as it was received and tested in Auntie Annie's very own kitchen!

THE LAST MERINGUE—
BLUE AVENGER'S WEEPLESS WONDER
LEMON MERINGUE PIE

For the crust, put in a bowl 1 cup flour and ½ teaspoon salt. Cut in 6 tablespoons shortening. (You do this with a curved multibladed tool called a pastry cutter.) When the largest pieces of shortening in the bowl are the size of small peas, add 2 tablespoons ice-cold carbonated beverage or plain ice water if that's all you have. Stir this mixture by sort of pressing it against the sides and bottom of the bowl with the back of a large spoon. When it all sticks together in a ball, take it out of the bowl and squeeze it into a harder ball. Roll it out with a rolling pin on a cloth or bread board that you have first sprinkled with a small amount of flour. When it's all nice and flat, press it into a 9-inch deep-dish Pyrex pie plate (the kind with the fluted edge) and trim off the excess. (You can eat the trimmings!) Press the pastry in with your thumb around the top in the fluted part so it sticks to the plate, and then puncture holes all over it with a fork, about 25 times, including the sides. Bake in a 425-degree oven for 9 to 12 minutes or until it's slightly brown.

For the lemon filling, mix 1 cup sugar and ¼ cup cornstarch in a medium-sized pot with a nice thick bottom. Add 1½ cups cold water and stir it around until completely smooth. Get 3 egg yolks (separate them from the whites) and beat them up a little bit in a small bowl. Then add them to the pot with the other stuff. Beat again gently with the eggbeater for a few seconds until it's all mixed up, but don't overdo it. Now, cook this on the stove over medium heat until the mixture starts to boil, but keep stirring all the time. When it starts to boil, look at the clock and keep stirring and cooking for 2 minutes more. Take the pot off the stove and add 2 tablespoons butter or real margarine, 1½ teaspoons grated lemon peel, and ½ cup lemon juice. Stir it all up real good and pour into your baked pie shell. Put plastic wrap over it and put the pie in the refrigerator.

For the pre-meringue, you have to mix 1¾ teaspoons Knox unflavored gelatin and 1 tablespoon cornstarch in a small pot. Add 2 tablespoons cold water and stir it up good until all the lumps are gone. Then add ½ cup boiling water, and cook at medium heat until it starts to boil, and then cook for 1 minute longer. Be sure to keep stirring the mixture all the while.

Remove from the heat and stir in ⅓ cup sugar and 1 teaspoon vanilla. Then pour this stuff into a small bowl and put it in the refrigerator. Set your timer for exactly 15 minutes.

Now do the meringue. As soon as the timer rings, take the pre-meringue mixture out of the refrigerator and start the meringue. Put 3 egg whites and ¼ teaspoon cream of tartar in a medium bowl and beat at high speed until it stands up in peaks when you raise up the beaters. (Be sure to shut them off before you raise them up!) Add the pre-meringue mixture in little dollops with one hand while you hold the beaters in the other. Keep beating after it's all mixed in until the meringue stands up in peaks again and looks like whipped cream. Then pile it gently on top of the lemon filling and spread around, being sure it touches the edges of the crust, or the topping will shrink up to about the size of a saucer. Make it look like a regular meringue pie you see in the bakery. Bake the pie in a 350-degree oven for 13 to 18 minutes or until it looks nice and light brown, like a meringue should. Do not bake too long. Remove the pie from the oven and put it right into the refrigerator. (Put a towel under it so it won't crack the refrigerator shelf.) After it gets cold, you can cover the pie with another deep-dish pie plate just like the one it's in. Try not to cut into this pie for at least 4 hours. The pie should be nice and cold before you eat it, and it is absolutely guaranteed not to weep, ever! You have Blue Avenger's word on that!

Blue Avenger had just made lemon meringue pie history. Oh, wow! Another dream come true. But the best was yet to come.

The city council chambers were jam-packed, and angry citizens were standing in the corridors and blocking the doors, driving the fire marshals mad. It was seven forty-five on Monday evening, the thirteenth day of February, and the meeting had not yet been called to order. The steady hum of voices was rising ever louder, and the crowd was getting mean. Fourteen more shootings had occurred over the weekend, and no one felt safe anymore, no matter how many guns they owned.

"Testing, testing, one, two, three—"

There was something wrong with the PA system. "Testing, testing, one, two, three—hey, it's okay now, sluggo! Run that mike over here!"

"Will everyone please take their seats? We can't begin until we get those aisles cleared. Come on, folks. Please, clear those aisles."

A young woman in a blue suit came up to the microphone and bent her head toward it like a turkey. "I have an announcement. Will Councilman Dwight Pinkerton please check with Doris Scopes. Dwight, please see Doris. She has found the folder. Repeat. She has *found* the folder." The woman in the blue suit smiled at the audience and gave a little wave. "Thank you," she said.

Blue Avenger, looking spectacular in his vest and towel, was seated off to the side and in back of his friend and new admirer, Dr. Milton P. Blankenship, who in turn was seated behind the long curved table with some of the other members of the council. Josh and Sally and Omaha and Margie were sitting in the second row, since they were almost the first to arrive.

"Where the *#%! is everybody?" Councilwoman Peters said loudly. "Let's get this *#%! show on the road!" She spotted Councilman Pinkerton talking to a television reporter along the center aisle. "Hey, Dwighty!" she shouted, for Councilwoman Peters was the bane of the elected members but the darling of the crowd. "Hey, Dwighty, get your *#%! on over here! We can't wait for you all night."

Dr. Blankenship purposely saved Blue for last. The

meeting had become a shambles. No new proposals had been offered, just the same old song and dance. More policemen on the beat. Metal detectors at the schools. Free classes in gun safety for the tiny tots. And finally Councilman Blankenship stood up to speak. It was nearly eleven o'clock.

"Before we break for the night," he began, "we have one more speaker on the agenda. I'd like to present to you the pride of San Pablo High and the newly crowned king of meringue—our one, our only *Blue Avenger!*"

Josh and Sally and Omaha and Margie jumped up and shouted, "Yay!" and of course the crowd went wild! (Scores of partially eaten weepless lemon meringue pies were at that very moment waiting to be consumed in refrigerators all over town, and dozens more had already been consumed!)

Blue stepped forward, confident but modest, with a debonair toss of his head and the barest hint of a smile. He held up his hands for quiet, and a hush fell over the crowd.

"Yeah, Blue!" piped up a voice from the rear just as he was about to speak.

The more vocal members of the crowd roared their

approval, again clapping and stomping their feet.

Once again Blue called for quiet, and then he began his speech. *"Guns don't kill people—"* he began, and the place was up in arms.

"Boo! Boo!" some hollered, because they were deathly sick of that phrase.

"Yeah! Yeah!" said others, because they dearly loved their guns.

Once more Blue held up his hands for quiet, and the crowd soon obeyed his command.

"No, guns don't kill people, *but bullets do!*"

While that was not exactly a new idea, at a time like this it was a confusing twist. But who could argue with that? Many friends and relatives of the recently slain were there among the audience, and they could certainly attest to the veracity of that precisely stated fact.

"So, my friends, the solution is obvious! Let's simply ban the bullets!" Blue exclaimed, with his innocent eyes opened wide and his arms extended toward the crowd.

"Fat chance!" someone hollered, followed by groans and catcalls and rude noises. And that's when Blue rose to his finest moment. Standing tall and motionless, facing the crowd, he again waited patiently for them to quiet down. Then he spoke directly into the microphone the simple words, "Winger Stingers."

Heads turned to one another. "What did he say?"

"Winger who?"

"I said *Winger Stingers*," Blue repeated, blue eyes blazing, "which are tranquilizing dart replacements for bullets that can be made to fit all existing guns!" He briefly filled them in on the Winger brothers' amazing invention and the newly improved tranquilizing solution.

"Just think of it!" he said. "Bullets can now be outlawed in Oakland! Naturally, the use of these darts under *unlawful* circumstances should be subject to severe penalties, but citizens can arm themselves with Winger Stingers instead of bullets for self-protection. The old I-need-my-gun-to-defend-myself argument will no longer hold water. Because actually," he added, "they can legally keep their guns. It's the *bullets* they'll have to give up!"

As preposterous as it sounded, the idea suddenly sprouted wings and took off. The fed-up men and women of Oakland, eager to try anything, stood up to voice their wholehearted approval, while the few die-hard gun toters in the crowd could see they were hopelessly outnumbered.

A plan of action was suggested and voted upon with surprising ease. A bullet-exchange period would be established, where citizens would trade in their old deadly bullets for the new Winger Stingers. Sufficient publicity, including house-to-house in-person notifications, would be conducted by a duly appointed committee of citizens. After the deadline, the sale or possession of bullets in the city of Oakland would be strictly prohibited. The penalties would be severe. Persons found guilty of possessing even one bullet after the prescribed date would face imprisonment for a term of one to five years, with absolutely *no television viewing or pizza* the entire time. The city of Oakland had finally had enough!

A few minutes after the council meeting ended that night, Blue had an extraordinary experience, one that he would remember all of his life. On the way out of the building, people had been crowding around him to pat him on the back and shake his hand, saying things like "Nice going, Blue!" and "Great job!" By the time they were in the parking lot the crowd had thinned out, but one elderly man walking a few steps ahead of him turned and waited for him to catch up. His mother and Josh kept walking toward the car, but Blue stopped when the old man started speaking to him. "I would never have believed the events I have just seen here tonight, son," he said, putting a hand on Blue's shoulder, "if I hadn't been here to witness them firsthand. What has happened here tonight is thoroughly out of the realm of reality. Utterly and totally unbelievable." The man smiled and shook his head, gave Blue a final pat on the arm, and walked away. As Blue stood there watching the old man disappear into the shadows, he suddenly had the feeling that he had ceased to exist. He literally could not move a muscle. He stopped breathing, and he couldn't even feel his own heart pounding. *Oh, no!* he thought. *It's happened. I'm not alive at all. I've turned into the real Blue Avenger! I'm nothing but a character in a comic book! None of this is really happening!*

Blue didn't know how long he remained in that state of uncertainty. Josh finally shook him out of it. "Come *on*, David!" Josh said, running back to get him. "What are you just standing here for? Mom says to hurry up!"

He was very quiet riding home in the car. His mother had offered him the keys before they got in, but Blue said, "No, you drive, Mom," and climbed into the backseat. He had a new dilemma to resolve, but it was just the kind of question that always intrigued him. When the answer finally came to him, he laughed out loud in pleasure. Of course he was not a comic-book character! Comic-book characters do not reflect on whether they are real or not! The very fact that he feared he might be one proved that he wasn't.

Or did it, really?

Even though it was after midnight by the time Blue got in bed that night, he just couldn't get to sleep. So he picked up *A Complete Travel Guide to Rome* from his bedside table and began to read. He read the brief summary of the history of the Eternal City and some hints on how best to survive when in Rome, and then came the descriptions of sights.

Blue read up to page twenty-two and then stopped to go get a drink.

If he turns the next page, what will happen? First, he will notice the photo, and immediately recognize the name of Giordano Bruno. Well, what do you know? he might say to himself. There's a statue of old George or Don Broomo himself!

So he will begin to read about the Campo dei Fiori: "one of Rome's most colorful squares, and the scene of a general market every morning, where you may buy anything from delicious cheeses and salamis to fresh fruit and vegetables. . . ." And on page twenty-three:

In the center of the *Campo dei Fiori* (meaning "field of flowers") there stands a haunting, brooding statue of Giordano Bruno, a sixteenth-century philosopher and heretic, who was burned at the stake on this very spot by the Inquisition on 17 February 1600 because he refused to recant his belief that the sun is the center of our planetary system and that the universe is infinite. Credited with inspiring the European liberal movements of the nineteenth century, particularly the Italian movement for national political unity, Bruno is also regarded by many as a martyr for the cause of intellectual freedom.

And then, if he turns the page, he will read this:

The faithful still gather at the foot of his statue on the seventeenth of February each year to solemnly commemorate the date of his death.

So there it would be, the missing piece of the puzzle. The $2,000 from Mrs. Laverne Livingstone of Austin, Texas, still sits unspent in Blue's bank account, an adequate amount for a round-trip plane ticket to Rome. Tomorrow is Tuesday, the fourteenth of February—three days before the ceremony in the Campo dei Fiori, just barely enough time left to arrange the whole thing! First, an official phone call from council member Blankenship to the passport office in San Francisco for a special one-day approval for Omaha's passport, then a Wednesday morning flight to Rome, a taxi ride from the airport directly to her hotel just a few steps away from the Campo dei Fiori and the brooding statue of Giordano Bruno. And then—on the following morning, among those gathered around the statue of the martyr—Omaha Nebraska Brown and her father who loves her dearly, Mr. Johnny Brown! Oh, what a glorious reunion it could be! But will it happen? The bringing together of a father and daughter, hinging on the turn of a page!

Blue, having made a trip to the bathroom and taken a drink, is at this moment climbing back into bed. He is sleepy now, really too tired to read anymore. So why does he reach for the book? What am I doing? he says to himself. Why don't I switch off the light?

Oh, no, his lips finally mutter the words. Is it time for *that* game again? Am I going to close my eyes when *I* choose, or am I merely part of some plan? Am I not the captain of my ship, am *I* not completely in control? So here we go testing, just one more time. I'll count to five and put the book down, snap off the light, and close my eyes. (Or will I?) *One, two, three—*

GET READY FOR THE STORM . . .

Harper tempest

An Imprint of HarperCollins*Publishers*

PRESENTS
CONTEMPORARY FICTION FOR TEENS

YELLOW BLUE BUS MEANS   0-380-73301-3
I LOVE YOU
by Morse Hamilton

CARE FACTOR ZERO   0-380-81390-4
by Margaret Clark

3 NBS OF JULIAN DREW   0-380-81098-0
by James M. Deem

TRUTH OR DAIRY   0-380-81443-9
by Catherine Clark

WELCOME TO THE ARK   0-380-73319-6
by Stephanie S. Tolan

THE ADVENTURES OF   0-06-447225-6
BLUE AVENGER
by Norma Howe

Available wherever books are sold.